Christmas in Canaan

Christmas in Canaan

Kenny Rogers
& Donald Davenport

HarperTrophy®
An Imprint of HarperCollins Publishers

Harper Trophy® is a registered trademark of
HarperCollins Publishers Inc.

Christmas in Canaan

Library of Congress Cataloging-in-Publication Data
Rogers, Kenny.
  Christmas in Canaan / Kenny Rogers, Donald Davenport.
—1st ed.
    p.   cm.
  Summary: In the early 1960s in a rural, racially charged Texas
town, a poor white boy struggling to get through school and a
book-loving black classmate find the common ground on which
to build true friendship.
  ISBN 0-06-000746-X — ISBN 0-06-000747-8 (pbk.)
  [1. Race relations—Fiction. 2. Family life—Texas—Fiction.
3. Texas—History—1951—Fiction.]   I. Davenport, Donald.
II. Title.
PZ7.R6357 Ch   2002   2001051747
[Fic]—dc21   CIP
                                                 AC

Typography by Andrea Vandergrift
❖
First Harper Trophy edition, 2004

Visit us on the World Wide Web!
www.harperchildrens.com

❖ ✱ ❖

*To Richard Brown, whose kindness alone
could easily fill a hundred small towns.*

—D.D.

Contents

Christmas 1975

"What's takin' them boys so long?" Daniel Burton wondered out loud as he stared impatiently out the kitchen window. "They only went to fetch a tree."

"They're not gonna come one minute sooner with you staring out the window like that," Sarah scolded. She brushed her hair away from her face with the back of her hand. "Don't worry. They'll come."

"I don't see why we gotta take a wrinkle pine over there in the first place. What's wrong with the wrinkle pine we got here? You've been wrapping presents and tying ribbons for days. I doubt there's room in this whole house to squeeze in one more angel. So why can't he come here for Christmas? Like before?"

Sarah ignored her father's question, focusing her attention instead on the row of gingerbread men and the mixing bowls filled with sticky white frosting, freshly shelled walnuts and dark, drizzling chocolate fudge. She loved Christmas. The way the house shone with candles and tinsel. The graceful sweep of red satin ribbons and strings of popcorn. More than anything, she loved the way the house smelled, the air warm and fragrant with ginger and nutmeg and cinnamon.

"Well, I think it's fine him wanting a tree of his own out there at Miss Eunice's his first Christmas home in eight years."

"Eight years? Can it really be eight years since he left Canaan?" Daniel shook his head slowly as he turned back to the window, letting his gaze wander past the empty fields to the rolling hills beyond. "And to think it all started with a thrashin'. A thrashin' between two little boys . . ."

Book One

Enemies

Chapter One

DJ and Rodney

The school bus lurched forward, sending DJ Burton offbalance and sprawling into the nearest empty seat. It was enough to cause Rodney Freeman to peek over the top of his book, surprised that the Burton boy had taken a seat so near the back of the bus.

The truth was, Rodney didn't mind sitting in the back of the bus; in fact, he liked it. He could settle into his usual corner, spread out his books and read. Miss Eunice, his grandmother, kept a farm on the outskirts of Canaan, the farthest point from town on the whole route, so there was always time to read. The bus was perfect for that.

There were no laws requiring Rodney Freeman or any other of the handful of black children be kept separate from the rest. The government had seen to that. But early that spring of 1960 what remained in the small town of Canaan, Texas, was an uneasy truce, a truce that served to hold the town together by separating the groups of people who lived there. Not that any of that mattered to Rodney.

Miss Eunice had surprised him with a copy of James Fenimore Cooper's *The Deerslayer* just the night before, a special illustrated edition, and even the unexpected arrival of DJ Burton and the grinding of gears as the bus got up to speed didn't warrant much more than a glance over the top of the cover.

DJ was big for his age, towheaded and with a broad face and eyes so pale blue they were almost gray. No sooner had he slouched into his seat than he began digging through scraps of paper in his book bag, searching for his unfinished homework.

"Hey, DJ, you still doin' homework?" Jimmy Ray Thompson asked, peering over the back of his seat.

"Yeah, well, how am I supposed to finish anything when my dad gives me chores till dark? And who asked you anyway?" DJ grumbled, hoping the others would see how busy he was and leave him alone. He hated always being the one kid in class who never had his homework done on time. He hated being called on to read in front of the others and hearing them snicker when he couldn't make out the words. Mostly he hated having to work so hard doing all those stupid chores for his dad on his stupid farm in a stupid town called Canaan.

He found his geography homework at the bottom of his bag. "What's the capital city of New York?" he read the question aloud and sighed. He could look up the answer, but the very thought of having to look up something that seemed like such common knowledge pained him. It was the kind of answer that deserved to be shared.

"Sarah!" he called to his sister. She was sitting with a clutch of girls her age near the front of the bus.

"What?" Sarah answered without turning.

He could see her ponytail bobbing as she chattered with her girlfriends and tried to ignore him.

"What's the capital of New York?"

"Look it up like you're supposed to," she said. Her voice was caked with such scorn, it sent her two friends into a fit of giggles.

Jimmy Ray turned in his seat to join the discussion.

"Why didn't you ask me?" he asked. Jimmy Ray considered himself a source of important information and was hurt he had been so easily overlooked.

"You know that?" DJ asked.

"I sure do. The capital of New York *is* New York." His voice rang with proud authority.

But the answer only confused DJ.

"Just New York?" DJ asked again. "Or New York City?"

"Either one," Jimmy Ray answered. "They're the same place."

Butch Waller shook his head violently in disagreement.

"They ain't the same," Butch argued. "One's a city and the other's a state."

"There's a New York that's a city, too," Jimmy Ray insisted.

"That's New York City," Butch insisted right back.

"Ah, you're crazy," Jimmy Ray muttered. "There ain't three."

DJ looked at his two colleagues with a growing helplessness. What had been a simple request to help him cheat on his homework had now escalated into a full-fledged discussion on geography.

"There's a plain New York that's a city, and there's a New York City that's a city and New York that's a state?" DJ was frustrated.

"No, Jimmy Ray don't know his butt from a beehive," Butch announced. "The plain New York is the only one that's a state."

"It's Albany." The voice came from somewhere in the back of the bus.

"What?" asked DJ, turning quickly in the direction of the sound.

"It's Albany," the voice said again.

Suddenly every face on the bus was looking in the direction of the voice, which came from behind the cover of *The Deerslayer*.

"What did you say?" DJ demanded.

Rodney Freeman lowered the book and looked out over the cover at the faces staring back at him.

"The capital of New York is Albany."

There was a brief silence, followed first by a giggle from one of Sarah's friends and then by a more malevolent snicker from Butch Waller.

"Hey, DJ, that colored boy's smarter 'n you."

DJ spun back around, the first flush of red beginning to creep up his neck like the mercury in a storefront thermometer.

"H-h-he ain't smarter," DJ stammered. "He just thinks he's smart. He's guessing, that's all."

It wasn't so much that the boy knew the answer; DJ had his doubts about that. It wasn't even that he was one of "them back of the busers," at least not entirely. More than anything else it was the fact that this scrawny kid, who didn't do a thing except read all day, was so confident about the answer.

"That's a pucky pile," DJ snarled at Rodney. "How do you know the capital of New York is Albany?"

"My grandma told me, that's how."

"I ain't never heard of your grandma and I ain't never heard of Albany." Then, DJ took up his pencil and began to write on the crumpled sheet of homework paper, saying the words out loud as he wrote them, as if he were chiseling them in stone. "The . . . capital of New York . . . is New York City."

"That's wrong," said Rodney. He screwed his face into a wicked little smirk before it again disappeared behind the book. "Don't blame me if you're too stupid to get the right answer even when you're cheating."

"I guess we'll hafta see," DJ announced. "We'll see who's stupid," he repeated, under his breath, for good measure.

Raising his rifle hastily to his shoulder, he took sight and fired. . . . The buck merely shook his head at the report of the rifle and the whistling of the bullet, for never before had he come into contact with man; but the echoes of the hills awakened his distrust, and leaping forward, with his four legs drawn under his body . . .

Wham!

The fist came out of nowhere, catching Rodney squarely in the solar plexus and knocking him to the ground, along with his brown-bag lunch and the cherished copy of *The Deerslayer*. DJ had been hiding behind the old elm that grew in the far corner of the schoolyard where Rodney always headed during noon recess. He had waited until Rodney buried his face in the book before launching the attack.

"That's for callin' me stupid." DJ towered over the other boy, who rolled on the ground, gasping for breath. "And this is for doin' it in front of everybody." He brought a foot down on the brown paper bag and ground it with his shoe until the sandwich and the sweet potato pie were nothing more than paste.

Drunk with vengeance, DJ surveyed the scene for other targets of opportunity, and his eyes fell on the book. Quickly, he snatched it off the ground.

"And this is for actin' so smart for a colored . . ." He took the book with both hands, opened it in the middle to rip it apart and came face to face with the colorful drawing of Natty Bumppo, the crafty old Deerslayer himself. He stood ramrod straight, the stock of his rifle pressed against his cheek, drawing a bead on whatever wild thing threatened just beyond. Something about the look in the Deerslayer's eyes, so brave in the face of danger, made DJ pause in his mission of destruction. He had never seen a rifle like that. A flintlock. And clothes made of buffalo hide and deerskin. That's how a real frontiersman dressed, not in boots and overalls. If only he could dress that way—he was sick and tired of wearing overalls and plaid shirts. If he could find a way to dress himself in buffalo hide and deerskin, what would it matter if he didn't know the capital of New York?

So distracted was he by the Deerslayer, DJ forgot all about the fight until Rodney rammed him in the belly with his head so hard that it knocked him down. Rodney struggled to free the book from his grasp, which only made DJ grip it tighter.

"Give it! Give it, you dumb, stupid . . ." Rodney growled. The two boys rolled and struggled on the ground until Rodney, reaching as far as he could, landed both hands on the back cover and pulled. DJ, both hands firmly on the front cover, pulled as hard or harder. What happened next would have made King Solomon proud, for the book ripped cleanly down the center of the spine.

Stunned, each boy looked at his half of *The Deerslayer*, as if somehow they had murdered a living, breathing thing. But if either of them believed separate but equal portions of the book represented justice in this particular struggle, he was about to get a lesson in civics.

Rodney flew at DJ with the murderous fury of an east Texas tornado. The first blow landed squarely in DJ's eye, and he yelped in pain. Rodney kept coming at him, skinny arms swinging wildly, drawing mostly air, until finally he had to slow down just to catch his breath. That's when DJ saw his opening.

Reaching back, he let loose with a right cross that connected squarely with Rodney's nose, staggering him like a hunter's shot grazing a twelve-point buck. To DJ's surprise, the scrawny kid looked dazed but he didn't go down.

They faced each other, both breathing heavily. DJ

rubbed his eye, and Rodney wiped away the trickle of blood from his nose. Then, simultaneously, their eyes fell on the only real casualty of the war, the two halves of the book. They eyed them for several moments, using the time to catch their breath. Finally, Rodney broke the silence.

"You couldn't read it anyway," he said.

That did it. Within seconds, both boys were rolling on the ground, punching and grabbing and raising such a cloud of dust that before long every kid on the playground had come running, followed quickly by Miss Herne, the teacher.

"Stop it. Stop it this instant," she yelled, her voice all but drowned out by the cheers of the kids, who hadn't seen such a good fight since Jimmy Ray stole Laura Tupper's milk money as a joke and she knocked out his front tooth. Bravely putting her own safety at risk, Miss Herne reached into the pile and grabbed each boy by the arm, yanking him to his feet. With one on each side of her, she marched them back to the schoolhouse like prisoners of war, followed closely by a column of children eager to see what might happen next.

Forgotten at the battle site, *The Deerslayer*, now a two-volume set, lay next to the flattened brown-bag lunch. Nearby rested a final artifact—a piece of paper, deeply creased, which had fallen out of DJ's pocket. It was his homework, with the teacher's ugly red X over DJ's scrawl, nearly obliterating the words "New York City."

William Jennings Bryan Grammar School was fronted by two wooden benches. Separated only by the school flagpole, they faced the little green square of sod that Miss Herne dutifully watered every morning. For DJ Burton, who sat on one bench, and Rodney Freeman, who sat on the other, the distance that separated them was beyond measuring—certainly not a few feet.

The boys waited in stone silence, looking straight ahead as around them the air was filled with the muffled recitation of multiplication tables, all the way up to the six times sixes. It might have gone higher yet, but the approaching rattle of Daniel Burton's pickup truck drowned out the rest. It shuddered to a stop in front of the benches, creaking and groaning like a tired old man.

It didn't take DJ long to plead his case.

"It was him who started it," he insisted, pointing at Rodney without bothering to look at him. "Him and his big mouth."

Daniel Burton, his shoulders broad from working in the fields, his face open and honest, cut him off with a simple nod of the head. "You best wait here."

DJ watched his father walk the short distance to the schoolhouse, poke his head through the open door and disappear inside. A minute later Miss Herne appeared, and the two of them talked on the porch. DJ tried to make out what they were saying, but their voices were purposefully low, and after a little while he gave up trying. Besides, it didn't much matter what they said. He knew what lay in store for him.

He chanced a look over at Rodney, who sat bolt upright, staring straight ahead.

"Don't even care if my daddy whups me. I'd do it again jus' to teach ya. You thinkin' you're so smart and all."

Rodney ignored him, although it was obvious he

heard, which only made DJ madder.

"So what if you're smart? So what if you read all them books? You're still just poor coloreds, and you'll never be as good as us."

Daniel Burton couldn't believe his ears. Obviously DJ hadn't heard him approach, and the boy was already in enough trouble just for fighting without saying something so hateful in front of his father.

"You'll never be as good as us even in a hundred million years."

A strange look crossed Daniel Burton's face. It was as if he were hearing someone else talking, not DJ. Not the boy he had always taught to be respectful, to live by the Golden Rule. These words belonged to someone else, and Daniel strongly suspected who.

Most of the way home to the farm they rode in silence, with only the rhythm of tires on the rough asphalt marking time. Fields of feed corn and milo and alfalfa sped by in various shades of green, bordered by thick stands of scrub pine and hickory.

Finally, Daniel broke the silence. "You ever have trouble with that colored boy before?" he asked.

"No, sir."

"Then why this time?"

DJ thought for a second and sighed. It was a lot of things, things that were hard enough to admit to himself, let alone to his father. How could he tell his father the trouble he had reading? No matter how hard he tried, the words always looked strange. How could he admit that most of the time he *did* feel stupid and sometimes felt he could never learn? It wasn't just Rodney. But then again, Rodney didn't have to tell the whole bus what he had been hoping no one would notice. No, that colored boy didn't have to tell the whole world how stupid he was.

"Awww, he thinks he's so smart just 'cause he knows things."

"Maybe he does. What kind of things does he know?"

DJ sighed again and turned to look out the window. "The names of places. Stuff like that. The names of cities." Suddenly he turned back to Daniel. "Ain't it bad enough I got to go to school with 'em?" he asked angrily.

Daniel thought for a second before answering. "Sounds like you've been talking to Earl," he said finally. "You say this boy's so smart? Maybe you'd learn something if you'd listen instead of fighting. Ever think about that?"

"I reckon there's nuthin' worth learnin' from the coloreds," DJ answered, again turning to the window.

"That right?" his father asked. "Nuthin' worth learning from them folks?"

"Yeah," DJ said. "Nuthin'. Completely nuthin'."

Chapter Two

Miss Eunice

*M*iss Eunice Freeman lived well beyond the outskirts of Canaan in a house that had been built by her late husband's father before the turn of the century. He had homesteaded the farm, and it had not been an easy go. The land had many more hills in those parts, and the soil was much less fertile. But it was the only land available to them. The folks in the government land office in Canaan had made that clear nearly a century before. It had taken Eustus Freeman and, later, her husband, Matthew Freeman, years of hard work to tame the land and nourish the soil enough so that the beans and corn and beets and yams they planted would grow.

The house was a simple white frame house, clean and neat. Like most things built with care by the owners, it had been constructed to last and had weathered the blistering summers and freezing winters with quiet strength. So what if it needed a new coat of paint? At sixty-eight years old, Eunice didn't have a mind to do much painting anymore, and the job would have to wait until Rodney got a little bigger. There really wasn't any hurry.

Behind the house was the family garden, and the years of care and tending were beautifully manifested in the neat rows of corn and the snap beans, green and healthy, hanging on their trellis. Rows of Beefsteak tomatoes, just beginning to set, would soon weigh down the vines in heavy red clusters. A patch for squash and melons was decorated with large floppy blossoms, which the bees visited before heading back to the hives Miss Eunice kept in the field beyond. The hives produced enough honey to make the bread Miss Eunice baked every Wednesday taste sweet as summer. Behind the garden was a small orchard of apple and apricot trees and beyond that a huge black walnut tree, providing the perfect shade for a hot afternoon.

It should have been just another peaceful morning as Daniel Burton sat in his pickup truck at the spot where Miss Eunice's driveway met the county road, but he was feeling anything but peaceful. In the small hours of the morning the germ of an idea had come to him as he lay in bed playing back the day's events. The plan had seemed simple, perfect. But now, as he sat staring at the Freemans' farmhouse, the truck idling impatiently, he wasn't so sure.

Maybe it was better to punish DJ as he always had, as his father had punished him, and his father before: a few healthy smacks with a fresh-cut switch from a sapling and a month of extra chores on weekends. That was certainly adequate punishment for most things a boy might do, like stealing something from the general store on a dare or breaking something through carelessness—all sins that he, Daniel, had committed at one time or another. But a broken window could be fixed; a stolen magazine could be paid for. This, somehow, seemed very different. How do you punish a boy for hating another?

Maybe it was impossible, but he knew he had to try.

Taking a deep breath and letting it out slowly, he dropped the pickup into gear and headed down the long driveway that led to Miss Eunice's house. The front door stood open, so Daniel knew somebody must be nearby. Knocking gently on the screen, he called.

"Miss Freeman?"

He waited what seemed like a reasonable time and knocked again, this time a little louder. When there was still no answer, he crossed to the edge of the porch that afforded a view of the garden.

"'Tis so sweet to trust in Jesus, just to take Him at his word . . ." Her voice was husky and there wasn't much of a tune to it, but the words were sung with feeling. "Just to rest upon His promise, just to know 'Thus sayeth the Lord.'"

Encouraged, Daniel followed the singing and soon saw Eunice Freeman, her face shaded by a wide-brimmed hat, picking snap beans from rows of neatly trellised vines. She continued to sing as she worked and, not wanting to startle her, he waited until between verses before he spoke.

"Miss Freeman?" he said.

She looked up suddenly, shading her eyes. He saw her stiffen, as if by reflex. Seeing a white man standing in her garden would do that, he supposed, and he smiled, hoping that would put her at ease. She put down the woven basket she carried on her hip, now nearly full of snap beans, and turned to face the stranger. She watched him cautiously.

"You ain't from the school. I can surely see that."

"No," he said, "not from the school. Just a neighbor. Daniel Burton."

Miss Eunice studied his face. It was an honest face, used to laughter, to kindness.

"I know you, surely, now's I get a look at'cha. Well, whadda you want comin' here?" she asked.

"I'd like to talk to you," Daniel said.

"Talk? Talk about what?"

Daniel smiled. "I reckon we need to talk about our boys."

The day had turned so unseasonably hot and humid, it seemed even the bluebottles had given up buzzing. Miss Eunice and Daniel Burton settled in the shade on the porch. Between them was a bucket full of cool well water and a wooden dipper so that they could replenish the Mason jars they used for glasses. Despite her hospitality, Miss Eunice was working up a head of steam. Now that she knew who Daniel was and why he had come, she was in no mood to send him off down the road without first giving him a little taste of the gospel according to Eunice Freeman.

"And the next thing I know, here he is with his clothes all tore up and his nose ableedin'. And fo' what? Jus' fo' tryin' to help your boy with his homework."

"My boy says your boy called him names. DJ says he called him stupid in front of his friends," Daniel replied calmly.

"My boy call your boy stupid?" she asked. "I've raised that boy myself, ever since his mama ran off when he was jus' a baby. I've raised him and I've taught him. He knows to work hard and he knows to mind his own business. To think my boy be callin' your boy stupid?" She shook her head, laughing to herself at the very idea. "Mister, you don't know my boy. You don't know my Rodney. No, sir."

"Some of the others heard it, too. Not just my boy."

A glimmer of anger flashed in Miss Eunice's eyes, the anger of a grandmother protecting her grandson, but also a smoldering collective anger—anger at how often the deck seemed stacked in favor of the high and the mighty, while the meek and the innocent inherited nothing but bad credit and rocky soil. While she would be the first to say she was never one to dwell on the pain and suffering of the past, she could not completely forgive and not entirely forget.

Miss Eunice drew deeply from her Mason jar. "Well, he knows now to stay away from yo' boy. He talks smart to yo' boy—or any other boy—I'll see to his whippin' myself."

"Seems to me," Daniel said, his voice soft and even, "that to keep from a whippin', your boy'll be afraid to even speak to my boy again. Ever. And my boy, the same thing."

"I 'laws that's true," Miss Eunice answered. "If that's how it be."

"Don't it seem that kind of punishment only drives them boys apart?"

"Still, a boy's gotta be punished," she said.

Daniel took a long drink of water and looked toward the horizon, where there were the beginnings of thunderheads. It had been a dry hot spring, and the land was thirsty for some rain.

"I've been thinkin' . . . ," he began, "what if we was to punish 'em by, instead of keepin' 'em apart, puttin' 'em together? Make 'em live together a whole week."

Miss Eunice threw him a look that said only the heat could make a man even consider such an idea.

"A week?" Her voice cracked with disbelief.

"Six days, then. Three days here. Three days at our place."

Miss Eunice's eyes narrowed as she looked at Daniel. "Your boy stay here?"

He nodded. "And your boy with us. Just like family. Treat him like we would our own boy."

Miss Eunice struggled out of her chair and walked the length of the porch, the boards creaking softly under her feet. For a long time she looked out over the garden. The breeze was just beginning to move through the corn, rustling the stalks.

"No, sir," she said. "It's nuthin' but a crazy idea, yo' boy coming here. Anyone can see there's barely room enough for the two of us as it is. An' if'n my boy goes to yo' place, who's gonna do his chores for three days while he's gone? How am I supposed to get along?"

Miss Eunice shook her head with slow determination. She probably could have thought up a dozen better reasons if she hadn't been interrupted by the sound of footsteps on the gravel path.

"Why, that's likely my boy now," she announced. She was suddenly pleased by the chance to show off to Daniel how a well-mannered boy behaved.

Rodney was on the porch before he even saw Daniel. He stopped, a frown crossing his face. He hesitated for a moment and then, without saying a word, crossed the porch and pushed through the doorway, slamming the screen behind him so hard it shook the whole house.

"Rodney?" Eunice exclaimed, her voice shrill with surprise and embarrassment. "Rodney, you get back here."

At first there was no response, and then Rodney's head appeared at the doorway.

"Rodney, this man's Mr. Burton. He's the other boy's father."

"Son," Daniel said, smiling and extending his hand.

The boy didn't move from the threshold of the door.

"I know who he is," Rodney said to Miss Eunice without taking his eyes off Daniel. He turned and disappeared into the house, slamming the door again, only to return moments later. This time he marched right up to Daniel, looking him full in the face.

"He is *too* stupid," he hissed like a hog snake startled from a nap. "You and that stupid boy owe me a new book."

Miss Eunice grabbed for the porch railing with one hand and with the other clutched at her heart.

"Rodney!" she cried again. "You jus' wait till I cut me

a hickory switch!" The only answer came from inside the house as another door slammed shut.

It was a long moment before Miss Eunice could even bring herself to face Daniel. She searched for words, nodding her head slowly as if the gravity of the decision were enough to crush her. "I suppose I could spare the boy a couple *two* days," she said.

"Then two days it is," Daniel replied, nodding in acceptance of the offer. "I reckon a boy can learn a lot in two days, Miss Eunice. Don't you?"

Chapter Three

The Punishment

lease don't make me!" DJ pleaded with his father.

They had driven over in silence, and now, as they sat in front of Miss Eunice's house, the horrible reality of the punishment was looming even worse than what he had imagined. DJ would have to stay with "those people," and just the thought of it brought him close to tears.

"I won't ever fight with him again. Never. Ever. I promise. Please, don't make me stay *here* with *them*."

Daniel looked into the face of his son, a face that only a day before had been filled with hatred; now it showed only fear. Not that the two emotions were all that different—one tended to lead to the other. It was only too easy to hate what made you afraid.

"I told Miss Eunice you'd help with the chores, just like at home," Daniel said, his voice calm but firm. "And I'm expecting you to get your homework done. Maybe you two boys can do it together. I figure that's part of what started this in the first place. But either way, I expect you'll do it. Understood?"

"Yes, sir," replied DJ, his voice small and dejected.

"Okay, then. Off you go."

But DJ wasn't going anywhere. He was hoping against hope that when it came right down to it, things would unfold like in the Bible, like the time the Lord commanded Abraham to offer up his son, Isaac, on the stony altar. Everyone knew the Lord didn't really want him to kill his boy and that the whole thing was only a test. All along DJ had been hoping that if he agreed to go along with the plan and was cheerful and cooperative, it would be considered punishment enough and he would be spared. But now his dollar's worth of faith was down to the last nickel. Could it be his father intended to sacrifice him after all?

A dark face appeared at the kitchen window. Then the front door swung open and there stood Miss Eunice, wearing a blue gingham apron. She stood motionless for several moments before being joined by Rodney, his face set hard with anger, no doubt feeling as persecuted by the arrangement as DJ.

"Go on," Daniel urged again. "They're expecting you for dinner."

DJ sighed. Like a convict trudging toward his own execution, he headed for the porch with slow, reluctant steps, dragging a worn leather grip with his things behind him.

Daniel climbed out of the cab and called out a greeting. "Evening, Miss Eunice. Evening, Rodney."

"Evening, Mr. Burton," Miss Eunice answered. Rodney simply glared, first at DJ and then at his father.

"I told DJ you'd give him chores," Daniel offered. "Boy's got the strength of a mule, so don't be afraid to put him to work."

"There's plenty fo' a strong boy to do around here," she said. "Plenty. Plenty. Don't worry 'bout that." She laughed at the very idea of anyone having to remind *her* that able-bodied boys should be put to work, which drew an immediate angry glare of betrayal from Rodney.

From the edge of the porch, DJ turned, giving one last pleading look toward his father, hoping that maybe the Lord would miraculously provide Daniel with an alternative sacrificial son. He waited in vain for that moment when Daniel would motion him back to the safety of the truck and together they would head home, joyfully reunited. But instead, Daniel gave one final wave.

"Be good, son. Make me proud" was all he said.

The rough pine table in the kitchen had been set for three, but there was scarcely room for two, what with dishes filled with snap beans and cut greens from the garden, a pan of freshly baked corn bread, and a large platter of some sort of meat smothered with dark rich gravy.

Miss Eunice set down the last of the dishes and struck a match to light the kerosene lamp. She carefully adjusted the wick to provide just the right light, a soft amber glow that curled around the edges of the table and made the small room seem even smaller. Then she sat and smiled across at the two boys, one hungrily eyeing the food, the other looking suspicious. Miss Eunice cleared her throat.

"In this house, we say grace fo' *every* meal," she announced. "So fold yo' hands 'n close yo' eyes shut 'n bow yo' head, just like Rodney there."

Rodney smugly folded his hands and tucked his chin down until it was nearly touching his chest.

Miss Eunice nodded her approval.

"There, now," she continued, carefully folding her own hands and bowing her head. "Thank you, Sweet Jesus, fo' us to share this meal one to the other . . ."

DJ squirmed in the hard wooden chair as the old woman poured out her thankfulness for everything in sight. Just having his eyes closed made him uneasy. What if saying grace was just a decoy, and while he sat there with his eyes faithfully closed, that crazy boy took his revenge? What fool would be sitting there in the presence of his enemies with his eyes closed? If he could just take a little peek to make sure everything was still all right, what would be the harm in that?

For Rodney, who knew the length of Miss Eunice's "company" prayers, grace still seemed insufferable. But there was something else. For all their recent history, it struck Rodney that he had never really had occasion to look at the other boy very closely, and he was suddenly curious.

"And bless them po' folk," Miss Eunice continued fervently, "them folk what ain't got themselves enough to eat, while we enjoy this plenty . . ."

Rodney cracked open one eyelid, barely enough to see, and then the other. The other boy had his head bowed, just like he'd been told, and his hands folded, and in that attitude of reverence he didn't look half so mean. Or so he thought until DJ opened both his eyes a crack and, for the briefest moment, there they sat, staring blankly in embarrassed surprise at each other while poor Miss Eunice blessed the rest of the world's lost and downtrodden. The two stared each other down.

The face-off would have continued had it not been for signs that the blessing was reaching a conclusion, and with that, both sets of eyes snapped shut and both heads rebowed as Miss Eunice built to a crescendo.

"As we eat this food, let us grow not only in strength but in love, one to the other, and a desire to be mo' like Thee. In the name of our Savior, Jesus. Amen."

"Amen," echoed Rodney, keeping his eyes closed a second longer so he could open them slowly, with ceremony.

DJ regarded the hypocrisy with disdain.

"You ain't the only ones to say grace," DJ protested. "My Daddy don't call it 'grace.' He calls it 'the blessing.'"

"'Tis the same thing, child," answered Miss Eunice gently.

"We gonna talk all night about prayin' or we gonna eat?" Rodney asked. Without waiting for an answer, he helped himself to a warm slice of corn bread.

All through dinner Miss Eunice found herself watching the table with a mixture of curiosity and concern, remembering that spring when clouds of grasshoppers descended on the garden and reduced everything to bare stems.

Whereas twenty minutes before the table had been filled with food, now about all that remained was a small piece of meat and a spoonful of gravy, and her eyes grew wider still as DJ headed for that with his fork.

"Where did a boy yo' size get hisself an appetite like that?" she wondered aloud.

"It's how I eat at home," DJ volunteered between mouthfuls.

Rodney, too, had been watching, and now the corners of his mouth tightened into a wicked hint of a smile.

"I didn't think you white folk had a taste for skunk," Rodney said.

DJ looked up from his plate, his mouth full.

"Skunk?"

Rodney nodded, his face brightly innocent.

"Fresh. Kilt it myself."

It took a second for the full impact to register. DJ staggered back from the table and bolted outside, nearly ripping the screen door off its hinges. From the darkness came the sound of retching, miserable and uncontrolled.

Rodney listened politely, his face a picture of concern. Finally he burst out laughing so hard he could barely keep himself upright in his seat.

"Rodney!" Miss Eunice scolded. "Why'd you tell him something like that fo'? Lucky I don't have my switch handy, or I'd blister you good."

Rodney tried to look at his grandma with an air of compassion, especially in the face of such a threat, as another wave of heaves echoed from the front of the house. Even Miss Eunice couldn't help but giggle a little, and the sight of her giggling made Rodney laugh all the harder.

"Will ya listen to that?" she declared, trying hard to muster a convincingly stern face. "'Tis shameful, boy. All that food goin' to waste."

Pushing back from the table, she hurried to the front door and opened it, calling out into the darkness. "Child? Child, he was jus' jokin'. That warn't no skunk. That was squirrel. Fresh squirrel. Kilt this very day."

The only answer from the darkness was a final, painful retch.

It was easy to forget just how quiet a simple house in the country could be, especially if it had been built without electricity or gas or indoor plumbing and, as a result, without the hums and buzzes and rattles of refrigerators and pipes in the walls. About the only sound DJ could hear besides a few lonesome crickets under the front porch was the noise made by Miss Eunice snoring lightly from her bedroom.

In his cramped bedroom Rodney slept like the dead, tucked comfortably under the quilt Miss Eunice and the other ladies in her quilting group had made. DJ sat stiffly upright on his side of the bed, as far away from Rodney as the narrowness allowed without putting himself in danger of rolling onto the floor.

There was no doubt that this was the worst part of the punishment. It had been bad enough to have to sit around the table and eat with those people, but the prospect of having to sleep in the same bed with Rodney was the last straw. He would stay awake every minute of each night, he would get his sleep on the bus or during recess, he would go without sleep entirely—anything other than having to admit that he had slept in the same bed with some colored boy.

At first staying awake had been easy. But as the hours began to roll by, DJ found himself becoming increasingly bored, and he knew boredom was the enemy because it was only one nod away from sleep. About that time he noticed the quilt, bright and detailed in the moonlight.

DJ had seen quilts before, but never any quite like this. The ones he had seen were mostly just colorful designs, but this quilt actually seemed to tell a story, the story of what it was like to live on a farm. With growing fascination he began to follow the story, tracing the images with his fingertips, from one square to the next, almost like reading a comic strip.

There were scenes of men planting, the fields rich and brown in the warm sun. Cows grazed peacefully while a fat tabby cat watched from a window. Next there were orchards heavy with apples while, in the field, men raced the first freeze to bring in the harvest. There were images of pumpkins and pies and jars of preserves, followed by a winter scene, the barn and fence posts stark against the drifted snow.

As DJ traced along with his finger, he stopped at one particular scene. A young black girl, a smiling girl with long pigtails braided with colored cloth, stood surrounded by brightly quilted sheaves of corn as if they could somehow protect her like a fortress. There was something about the image that captivated him. For a fleeting second, DJ imagined it was Miss Eunice, but the girl in the quilt seemed much too tall and, besides, Miss Eunice wasn't the kind of woman to waste a whole quilt telling stories about herself. No, this could only be one person—Miss Eunice's daughter.

Beyond the image of the girl, there were other panels. To get a good look, DJ leaned forward, and as he did, the bed—barely sturdy enough for one—rocked slightly. It was just enough to stir Rodney, who responded by pulling the quilt—and the story with it—tightly around him before drifting back off to sleep.

DJ shook his head dejectedly at yet another injustice to be suffered. Let the boy have his stupid quilt. He wouldn't be caught dead wrapping himself in something like that anyway. Sighing and straightening his back, DJ tried to settle in once more.

It figured to be a long night.

Chapter Four

The Girl in the Quilt

"**B**us is comin'," Rodney announced. DJ stood mindlessly pitching rocks at a fence post. He had tossed about a hundred rocks so far and hadn't even come close to hitting it.

"I got ears. I can hear it," DJ growled. It was obvious that even a breakfast of Miss Eunice's bacon and grits with fresh butter had not improved his mood.

His back was stiff from sitting up in bed all night and his stomach still felt a little queasy from that business about the skunk. But all that would pale in comparison to what was about to happen. The humiliation of facing

45

his friends and explaining he was being punished by having to move in with colored people—that was a fate far worse than eating a thousand skunks.

Dejectedly DJ crossed to the shoulder of the road, making sure to keep his distance from Rodney. He racked his brain one last time for a story that might somehow provide even the thinnest shred of cover. He considered coming up with a gripping tale of how he had been taken hostage by bank robbers who had left him for dead beside the very road that ran in front of Miss Eunice's farm, only to regain consciousness in time to hear the school bus.

He turned and pitched one last stone in the direction of the elusive fence post, hitting it solidly with a resounding *whack*. The trouble was, even if he could cobble together a good enough story, Rodney would know. And Sarah would know. And soon everyone would know that not only did he have to live with the Freemans but, on top of it, he was a liar, too.

The school bus lumbered to a stop, brakes protesting with a tired *screech*. DJ made a straight shot for an empty seat as far away from his friends as he could get, which wasn't far at all.

"Whatta y'all doin' here?" Jimmy Ray Thompson asked.

"Ask my dad. He made me."

"Made you what?"

"Spend the night," DJ snarled.

"Why?" Butch Waller slid over next to DJ, his freckled face round as the Texas moon and lit up with a mocking grin.

"It's my punishment for fighting," DJ answered. "Why'd ya think? For fun?"

"How long you gotta stay with 'em?"

DJ looked over at Jimmy Ray, who dissolved into a fit of laughter, rolling lengthwise on the bus seat.

"They gonna adopt you and raise you as one of their own?"

"You boys keep it quiet back there," Mr. Clancey yelled back over his shoulder.

"Two days," DJ grimaced. "Unless they poison me first."

47

Sarah was waiting patiently beside the road as the bus arrived at the Burton farm. She had been up in time to dress her baby brother and feed the others breakfast, set some beans soaking with a ham hock for dinner and still play shadowboard along the fence line nearly a dozen times before hearing the bus approach.

Shadowboard was a game Sarah invented, although it really wasn't much of a game. The morning sun shone through the fence posts, creating shadows, and the object was to run through the pattern, ponytail bobbing, careful to land only in the squares of sunlight—like hopscotch except more fun because the shadows changed with the seasons and sometimes there was mud or snow to navigate. She liked spring mornings best. The sun climbed higher in the eastern sky and made the patches of sunlight bigger and easier to land on.

DJ thought the game was stupid, and whenever he saw her play it, he told her how silly she looked. There was precious little time in her day for anything silly. Sarah had grown up early because the family needed her to. They depended on her. Just to have a few selfish moments to do something as silly as hopping on squares of sunlight without touching the edges always seemed glorious.

She quickly took a seat next to her friends. Before Mr. Clancey had shifted out of first gear, DJ was in the empty seat in front of her, turning to look pitifully at her, in his eyes the pain of one who has seen unspeakable misery.

"What's the matter with you?" she asked. "You look awful."

"She made us sleep in the same bed," DJ whispered.

"So? You afraid it'll turn you into one of them?" Sarah asked. "It's not catching."

Miss Eunice took Daniel at his word, and all day, while the boys were at school, she thought about what could be done around the place with a little extra boy power. By the time the bus dropped Rodney and DJ off in front of the Freeman place, she had compiled a respectable list.

They did some hauling and some lifting of heavy furniture so Miss Eunice could clean under it. They swept the porch and washed the windows. By late afternoon, the boys found themselves in the corn patch, chopping weeds that had taken root along the base of the stalks and were working the soil loose. Even that could make a difference in a drought year. For almost an hour the boys worked in silence, with only the sound of tools against dry earth and the rustle of cornstalks in the afternoon breeze.

"So how long *your* family lived in Canaan?" Rodney asked finally, more to break the silence than because he was truly interested.

"Since my great-granddaddy moved here," DJ replied. "Longer than you, I bet."

"Where'd he come from? Your great-granddaddy?"

DJ eyed the other boy suspiciously.

"How should I know?" he said. "Why you wanna know?"

Rodney shrugged. "No reason." He took to working at several weeds that had grown tall, chopping below the soil to get as much of the root as he could.

"I bet your kinfolk came from Wales, England," he said finally.

"And just how would you know to bet that?" DJ said, not even trying to hide the contempt in his voice.

"'Burton' is a Welchman's name. Same as Richard Burton the actor. He came from Wales."

DJ snorted his disgust, attacking a furrow with his hoe. The punishment was bad enough, but to have some colored boy tell him more about his family's history than he himself knew was just too much. What if he was right though? What if his family had come from England?

"I reckon maybe they did come from England. With Columbus. On the *Mayflower*," DJ announced, hearing the pride of his newly discovered pedigree blossom a little in his voice.

The other boy rested on his hoe.

"Columbus came from Spain, not England. And he was on the *Santa Maria*, not the *Mayflower*. And he'd been dead a hundred years before any of your relatives showed up, if they showed up at all."

DJ brought the blade of the hoe down with such force that it missed the weed he was aiming at and sliced through the base of a young cornstalk, which toppled slowly and landed neatly at Rodney's feet.

"So what kind of name is 'Freeman?'" he blurted out. "It sure ain't no Welchman name."

Rodney simply glared at DJ a moment before picking up the fallen stalk. He chopped it into several pieces and tossed them in the pile with the rest of the weeds.

"It's the name of an African slave," he replied simply.

DJ watched Rodney, trying to guess whether this was just another one of his jokes, like the roast skunk. But the way he said it, straight out, with a certain sense of pride, made him think he was probably telling the truth.

"Your great-granddaddy was a slave?" DJ asked. He tried not to act too interested.

"No, but *his* daddy was," Rodney answered, stopping to look DJ in the eyes. "Come over on a slave ship from Africa to work the fields. His only name was Slave Man John." Rodney stopped, wiped the sweat from his face and took a long drink out of the water jar. "One day he heard that President Abe Lincoln had freed all the slaves, so he stood right up in the middle of that tobacco field and told the whole world he would never again be Slave Man John, but Freeman John, from that time on."

"Freeman John?" DJ repeated, without understanding.

"Because he was a *free man*. Freeman. That was his new name. John *Free*man," Rodney said slowly, letting the emphasis fall on the first syllable. "I guess you could say it's an American name."

Rodney bent down to pull away the last of the weeds. DJ watched him, feeling the tug between the intrigue of the story and the cherished resentment he'd been so rigorously tending. The resentment won easily. Surveying the garden, he snorted in disgust at the whole ridiculous notion.

"Well, all's I know is if your great-granddaddy's daddy grew tobacco like you said, how come I don't see no tobacco growin' around here?" DJ challenged him.

Rodney faced the other boy, sighed and shook his head ever so slightly.

"That was in Virginia," Rodney said. "Anybody knows

tobacco don't *grow* in Texas," he continued, adding under his breath loud enough that DJ couldn't possibly help but hear, "anybody that wasn't so *stupid. . . .*"

It was well past midnight, the house was quiet and even Miss Eunice's snoring was barely audible; but still DJ sat, ramrod straight in bed, his arms folded in protest across his chest. Beside him Rodney slept, the deep comfortable sleep that comes from three hours of chores followed by a fried chicken dinner topped off with two pieces of sweet potato pie.

DJ squirmed, stubbornly forcing himself to stay awake. For a while he concentrated on listening to the sounds of the night. Somewhere in the distance he could hear the persistent baying of a hound, probably annoyed at a raccoon rummaging through the garbage. Farther off there was the mournful whistle of a locomotive, and DJ imagined himself hitching the slow-moving freight, bound for Arkansas and points beyond.

He glanced at Rodney's books, placed neatly on

shelves, so many they nearly covered the whole wall. He wondered what it would be like to pick out one of them and read it straight through without any help—especially the thick ones, so thick he couldn't imagine anybody ever reading them.

Rodney stirred in his sleep, and the quilt that had been tucked snugly around him flattened out, its brightly colored panels beckoning. Creeping slowly, DJ bent over the quilt, picking up the story where he had left off the night before.

From the look of things, something had come along that changed life dramatically. While before there had been the abundance of the harvest, now the panels seemed much more severe. The fields stood strangely fallow. The trees in the orchard bore hardly any fruit and, perhaps most important, something had happened to the young smiling girl.

She was older, Rodney could tell that. And her pigtails were gone. She stood, her back to the house, her arms crossed as if she had stubbornly made up her mind about something and wasn't likely to change it. There was something powerful and, at the same time, sad about her expression.

Intent on studying the face of the girl, DJ hadn't noticed what was in the background, pressed against the window of Miss Eunice's house. It was the small face of a baby, framed in the window, the window to the very room he found himself in. The baby's hand was reaching out toward the woman, but she appeared not to see it. Or maybe she didn't want to see it.

DJ stared at the image. It reminded him of his own mother and the last time he'd seen her as she left for the hospital in Clarksboro when his little brother was born. He remembered her standing in front of the house, shivering in the frosty morning air. DJ had watched her from the kitchen window, just like the boy in the quilt. One minute she was there, and then she was gone, leaving the rest of them behind to get through any way they could.

DJ rubbed his tired eyes. It was hard trying to make out the pictures in the quilt by the thin light the moon gave through the window. Even if he closed his eyes to rest them, it wasn't the same as sleeping. Then, to be a little more comfortable, he pulled the quilt up around him and sidled down in bed until he was nearly flat.

For a little while, his mind wandered back again to the last time he had seen his mother. He tried to hold the memory tightly, but bit by bit it softened into more of a dream than a memory, and by the time the hound in the distance finished baying, the memory had become purely a dream.

Chapter Five

Bandit

The house was named for DJ's grandfather, Wylie Jerrit, and it sat in the saddle of a knoll, guarded on either side by towering elms. It was the second house that had stood on that exact spot; the first had been built in the 1880s by Wylie Jerrit's father, but it had burned to the ground in 1926. Wylie had taken his time building the current house, doing most of the work himself. Over the years he continued to work on it, expanding it, adding bedrooms and framing out the porch behind the kitchen. The house had weathered good times and bad, births and deaths, and to Wylie it would always be the Jerrit house, even though he was the only Jerrit who still lived there.

Behind the house stood the barn, faded red and missing some boards. Each spring Wylie made plans to shore it up, but each autumn there seemed to be less money after the harvest than the year before, so the barn went unrepaired and unpainted. It was that way with farming.

Beyond the barn the land sloped down to a small thicket of cottonwood trees that huddled along a muddy little creek. On either side of the creek the brush grew so tall and thick in places, it would have been easy for a person to get lost. For three generations of Jerrit children, that had always been the magic of playing near the creek. But now the children who sat around the breakfast table or played along the creek and would someday grow up to own the Jerrit farm were not even Jerrits. They were Burtons.

It had seemed a blessing that Wylie Jerrit's only daughter should meet a man like Daniel Burton. He was the kind of young man Wylie had always hoped Betsy would marry. Honest. Respectful. Someone with a good, level head. Here was a young man who knew the value of hard work and could someday, perhaps, hold the farm together after Wylie was gone. Who could have guessed Betsy would die so young?

The school bus had barely pulled to a stop before DJ clambered down the stairwell, pounding impatiently for the doors to open like a convict being released from prison. Mr. Clancey hadn't time to turn on the flashers and set the parking brake before DJ scissored between the doors and disappeared down the gravel driveway toward home with long angry strides, leaving behind a forlorn-looking Rodney.

Rodney toyed with the idea of simply turning away, walking the couple of miles back to Miss Eunice's house and taking whatever punishment she would certainly dish out. It couldn't be worse than this. At least he could sleep in his own bed. However, she might make him come back and stay even longer. It was a thought so unpleasant, it was no wonder he jumped when he felt something brush his arm. Turning, he found himself face to face with Sarah.

Rodney had almost forgotten that the horrible bully who had ripped his clothes and ruined his book had a sister, but there she was, standing beside him, smiling the most reassuring smile. Sarah was nine, a year younger than DJ, and tall for her age.

"Not very nice leaving you behind like that," she said. "Sometimes he's a brat."

Rodney shrugged and looked down at his shoes, making a circle in the gravel with first one toe and then the other.

"I don't blame him," he said. "I didn't want him at my place, neither."

"It's not so bad," she said. She tossed her head in the direction of the house. "Come on. You'll see."

Together they walked toward the house as Sarah began to describe the people who made up her world.

"There's Papa," she said. "You've already met him. Don't be annoyed if he doesn't say too much. At least, not at first. Sometimes he thinks a long time before he says anything, but that's just his way. And then there's Wylie—he's my grandpa. Sometimes I think he *never* waits a second before he opens his mouth, and sometimes you'll swear he's the crabbiest man in the whole world, but underneath, he doesn't mean anything by it. And you know DJ."

"I know he don't like to eat skunk."

"Skunk?" Sarah asked, puzzled. "When did DJ eat skunk?"

"He didn't," Rodney answered flatly. "He just thought he did."

Sarah gave Rodney a puzzled look but he just smiled.

"Then there's my baby brother, Bobby," she continued, "but we call him Bobber. He's only four."

"Don't y'all have a mama?" Rodney asked.

Sarah shook her head. "She died. Right after Bobber was born. Eclampsia took her."

Rodney nodded as if he understood. "I don't have a mama, neither," he said. "But my grandma's like a mama."

"We do pretty good," Sarah said, a little surprised at

how protective her voice had suddenly become. "We all do a little to raise Bobber. Not exactly like a mother would raise him, but like a family would."

They approached the stretch where the gravel drive skirted the neighbor's property, running along the fence where Sarah played shadowboard each morning. They were so busy talking that they did not notice the shadowy figure who watched them from the other side of the fence, hidden by a small stand of cottonwoods.

Earl Hammer stood, his shotgun on his shoulder, watching and listening. His eyes widened as he spotted Rodney and then narrowed into slits. What in heaven's name could that fool Burton be thinking, allowing that girl of his to walk beside a colored boy?

There was something frightening about Earl. The way he sullenly watched the world around him. The sour expression on his face. The bitterness with which he would talk about people he didn't like—who, as the years went by, came to include nearly everybody.

For his part, Daniel always treated Earl kindly and urged the children to be respectful, like any good neighbor should. Twice a week Wylie headed over to Earl's to play dominoes in the evening. But no amount of neighborliness could overcome the bald fact that a cruel streak ran through him, sometimes near the surface, sometimes buried deep.

Most people blamed Earl's bitterness on Buddy, his son, and Buddy's troubles with the law. For all his years growing up, there was scarcely a person in Canaan who hadn't had something bent, broken or stolen by Buddy Hammer. Most people tried to forgive and forget, believing that underneath it all there must be some good to the boy. That was before he stole the preacher's car and drove it to Chicago. From there, it only got worse. There was an argument. A fight. And when it was over, one man lay dead.

Earl shook his head in disbelief as he watched Sarah and Rodney disappear into the Jerrit house. One thing's for sure, he thought, when ol' Wylie Jerrit comes over for dominoes, like he does every Wednesday, I'll give him a lesson in American history he'll never forget.

Reaching down, he pumped a shell into the chamber

of the Remington and, hitching up his pants, headed off to the creek, daring anyone or anything to be foolish enough to cross his path.

From where he stood, his back against the barn, DJ could just see the top of the cottonwoods along the creek, and the thought of hiding down there until dark seemed like the best idea he had come up with all day. Maybe he would just stay down there the rest of his life—live like a hermit, only coming out at night to hunt for food. No more multiplication tables, no more state capitals and, most of all, no more Rodney. He leaned his head back against the rough siding and closed his eyes. It was the happiest he had been all day, maybe all week.

The sound of footsteps cut short his reverie, and he looked up just in time to see Rodney coming around the corner of the barn, his hands full of windblown trash. Picking up all the paper down by the barn and along the fence was one of the chores Daniel had handed out to both boys. So far, Rodney was the only one who had done any actual picking.

DJ let him pass without saying a word. Then he reached into his pocket and found, crammed deep in the corner, an old wadded Juicy Fruit wrapper. With a casual flick of the wrist, DJ launched it squarely into Rodney's path. For once his aim was perfect; it bounced twice and came to rest right between Rodney's shoes.

"Missed one," DJ said.

Rodney picked it up, walked over to DJ and dropped it at his feet.

"So did you," Rodney replied, screwing his face into the same dirty little smirk he had given DJ on the bus.

DJ felt the anger rising in his body. He knew he was much stronger than the other boy, and with nobody around to break it up, he could whip him but good. Maybe that would wipe the smirk off his face once and for all.

"We're only picking up trash because you're here," DJ said, his teeth gritted. "It's 'make work.'"

"How could it be 'make work' for you? You ain't picked up nuthin'."

"Well, you hate it so much, why don't you quit?" DJ said, his voice menacing. He could feel his hands balling up into fists. All it would take was one more smart remark, one more little smirk. Or maybe not even that. "Huh?" DJ challenged him. "Why don't you just quit?"

Rodney stared into the face of his rival. "'Cause I ain't like some lazy . . . fool . . ."

DJ grabbed Rodney by the front of the shirt and felt his right fist harden like a rock as he cocked his arm back, ready to hit this boy harder than he had hit anything in his whole life. But in that split second before he unleashed his fury, something stopped him. Stopped them both. Cold.

It was a gunshot. It came from somewhere down in the thicket along the creek and was followed by the sound of a wounded animal yelping in pain.

Both boys turned at the sound and stood listening, fists still raised.

"What was that?" Rodney asked.

"Dunno," DJ said, scanning the thicket for any sign of movement.

"Think someone's dead?"

"Dunno," DJ replied again. "But I'm gonna find out."

Off he headed in the direction of the shot, dogged closely by Rodney. Together they crossed the rolling pasture and approached the thick growth along the creek. DJ stopped and motioned for Rodney to keep still.

There was something moving through the underbrush, moving with heavy methodical steps, right toward where they were standing.

Quickly DJ scanned the area for cover. Behind him was a lone scrub pine, looking forlorn and out of place among the cottonwoods and creek willows. It wasn't very big, but it was low to the ground and bushy enough to provide some cover.

"Behind the tree," DJ whispered, pointing toward the pine, and the two boys huddled in close, pressing themselves against the scratchy needles, trying to catch their breath.

For a while DJ cupped his hands behind his ears, listening carefully.

"Hear 'im?" asked Rodney in a whisper.

DJ shook his head. "Nope. He's stopped."

A bird called a shrill warning. Both boys turned back toward the direction the footsteps had come from and waited, listening intently for any sound. Again the bird cried its warning. Still they listened, imagining every little sound to be the sound of a footstep on a dry twig and every rustle the sound of a killer working his way silently through the brush.

After what seemed like an hour, there were no more sounds, and Rodney began to relax. That's when he felt the large rough hand grip his shoulder like iron.

He let out a yelp and spun around, twisting to get away from the figure who towered over him.

"Well now, who's our little friend here?"

Earl Hammer held Rodney with one hand and the shotgun with the other.

"He ain't *my* friend," DJ sputtered, protesting.

"He ain't, ain't he?" Earl replied, his gaze never leaving DJ. "If I was him," he said, nodding in the direction of Rodney, his face dark and threatening, "I'd be careful about sneakin' around back in the woods. Especially these particular woods." He turned to Rodney and gave him a crooked smile, revealing a stubby row of stained teeth. "Would be a shame to accidentally mistake you for some thieving varmint. You understand, boy?"

"Yes, sir," Rodney heard himself respond, though he wasn't at all sure how he found enough voice to say it.

Earl nodded, pleased that he had achieved some noble breakthrough in human understanding and, with that, he ceremoniously released his grip on Rodney's shoulder.

"I finally got that sonuvabitch coyote that's killin' my chickens." Earl turned to DJ and smiled the same crooked smile. "So that's one less varmint at least."

He looked at Rodney, arched his eyebrows and smiled a final time before abruptly turning and heading off, his gun resting on his shoulder, pausing only once to turn back and look at the two boys before he disappeared over the knoll. DJ and Rodney watched him go. It wasn't until they were sure he had really gone that they actually began to breathe again.

"Scared me near to death." Rodney slumped to the

ground, as if he himself had been shot. "Who's that?"

"That's Earl Hammer. He's just mad 'cause his boy's in prison for killing a man," DJ added. "Earl says only reason they locked him up was on account it happened up North. The other man was colored. Down here, nobody'd done nuthin'."

Before Rodney could answer, from the heavy underbrush along the creek there came a cry, the cry of an animal in pain. Varmint or not, whatever it was that Earl had shot, he hadn't shot it dead.

The boys looked at each other, wondering if each was thinking the same thing as the other.

"Wanna go find it?" DJ asked excitedly.

"Think we could?"

"Sure. I used to make forts in that thicket all the time. Come on."

Spring had been unusually dry that year, and the creek had nearly disappeared. Only a few stagnant pools remained, smelling like sulfur and covered with thick yellow scum. Cottonwoods and creek willows crowded the banks for moisture, which made it hard to follow the creek bed.

The boys searched along the bank, stopping often to listen for any sound from the wounded animal, but whatever had made the cry was now silent.

"Why don't we track it?" Rodney whispered. "Like Natty Bumppo."

"Who?"

"Natty Bumppo. The Deerslayer. He could tell whether it was a buck or a doe just from lookin' at the track. An' if it was a buck, he could tell if it was a ten point or a twelve by the tore up branches overhead."

"Well, you can look at all the branches you want, but that wasn't no deer Earl shot, and whatever it was, it didn't leave no tracks I can follow."

They resumed the search, but after twenty minutes of tramping through the brush, DJ was growing tired. It would be dark soon, and dinner would be ready. Whatever Earl had shot hadn't made a sound for so long, it was probably dead anyway. As he turned to call to Rodney, something caught DJ's eye. Lying on a bare gravelly patch of creek bed was something shiny. Even from a distance, DJ knew what it was—a spent shotgun shell from Earl's Remington.

Crossing to it, he gave a quick look around. From the place where Earl had fired, the thicket crowded in on three sides, leaving only a small clearing straight ahead. Whatever Earl had shot would likely be in there.

"You stay here," he called to Rodney. Deliberately, a step at a time, he headed for the clearing, trying to walk as straight a line as he could from the spot of the shotgun shell.

DJ had gone no more than fifty feet when suddenly he dropped to his knees. Grass stalks had been freshly broken, and that wasn't all; as he peered closer, he saw what he had been hunting for. Clinging to one stand of creek grass were a few bright drops of fresh blood.

DJ motioned for Rodney to advance and together they huddled around the place where the animal had fallen. From that spot, a trail led into the brush. The grass had been matted down in other places, and every so often there was another spot of blood, glossy red against the green of the creek grass.

DJ pointed to a break in the grasses that led farther down the bank of the creek, into an area of overgrown willows.

"Come on," he whispered.

Even on their hands and knees, DJ and Rodney could barely crawl under the thick, stubborn undergrowth, but the trail was unmistakable. There were more spots of blood, much closer together. Whatever came through was moving more slowly—or bleeding more heavily—by the time it had gotten here.

Suddenly DJ stopped and put his finger to his lips. The boys stood stone quiet, listening. For a long time there was nothing, and then they heard a low whimper, so close it could have been right beside them.

It came from a small hollow hidden by a canopy of twisted brush only a few paces away. DJ's first instinct was to head straight for the sound, but it took only a second to reconsider. Instead, he fished his pocketknife out of a pants pocket and picked up a small cottonwood branch.

Wounded animals, even ones that are badly hurt, can still be dangerous.

With DJ leading the way, the boys crept forward, trying not to make a sound until finally they crouched directly above the hollow. Inside they could hear something breathing. The breaths were shallow and made a rasping sound.

Gathering his courage, DJ lay down and peered inside.

"Well, I'll be switched," he whispered.

"What is it?"

"It's a dog. Damned ol' fool Earl Hammer shot hisself a dog."

"Let me see," Rodney said, inching on his belly until he was side by side with DJ.

The dog was little more than a puppy, chocolate brown with a patch around his neck that made it look like he was wearing a white bandanna. In the middle of his chest was an ugly red stain.

"He's just a pup," Rodney exclaimed.

"Let's get him out of there," DJ said, lunging as far as he could. Before he had even laid a hand on the puppy, Rodney yanked him back by the shoulders.

"Whatta you doin'?" DJ snapped.

"You want to kill him?" Rodney snapped back. "You move him wrong, it'll kill him. He starts thrashing around, he'll tear hisself up."

"How we supposed to move him, then?"

Rodney thought for a moment. "We've got to *immobilize* him," Rodney concluded. "Give me your shirt."

Without thinking, DJ started unbuttoning his shirt but stopped after the third button, looking at the other boy suspiciously.

"What's wrong with your shirt?" he asked.

"Mine's better for the compress," Rodney announced. He had already taken off his shirt and folded it into a small neat square. Moving slowly on his hands and knees, he approached the pup.

The dog didn't move, other than to lift his head slightly and set it back down with a whimper almost too soft to hear. Gently Rodney took the tightly folded square of fabric and pressed it over the wound. Holding it there with one hand, he reached his other hand back for DJ's shirt.

Folding it lengthwise to make a sling, Rodney wrapped the sleeves around the pup and tied them in such a way that they would hold the compress in place and also keep the dog from moving.

Backing his way out of the hollow, Rodney turned to DJ.

"You can pick him up. But careful now. Put your arm down the middle of his belly so that his head is in the crook of your elbow. That way, he can't move."

Carefully DJ inched toward the dog and, taking care to do just as Rodney had instructed him, slipped one arm underneath the puppy to pick him up. It wasn't easy but DJ moved slowly, deliberately, careful always to support the pup with an arm underneath.

Once out, the boys turned quickly for home, moving as steadily as they could through the creek bottom, up through the thickets that lined the banks and finally across the rolling pasture that led back to the Jerrit farm.

Daniel had cleared out a small stall in one corner of the barn, and Sarah had arranged fresh straw and placed the pup on some clean towels. The boys had strung together a work light, positioned low, so there would be a little warmth in case the barn got drafty during the night.

The pup lay on its side, its wound having been cleaned and dressed with gauze. Only the slow rise and fall of its chest gave any sign that the animal was still alive.

DJ and Rodney sat on a straw bale, wearing old sweatshirts Sarah had brought them, while she tried to soak the blood out of their school shirts.

"I doubt you'll see a change before morning," Daniel said from the door of the stall. "You boys need to get to bed. You've got school tomorrow."

"Can't we sleep here? In case?" DJ pleaded.

"Yeah, just in case?" Rodney echoed.

Daniel looked in the two faces, faces that only hours before had been hard and angry. Now they were bright and hopeful. He felt his resolve weaken and, for once, he didn't mind.

"You ain't gonna run home and tell Miss Eunice I made

you sleep in the barn, now, are you?"

"No, sir." Rodney shook his head slowly.

"And your school work's all done?"

"We can do it here. Under the light," DJ insisted.

"You can get yours done, too?" Daniel asked Rodney.

"Did mine on the bus," Rodney replied, then quickly added, "Most of it, anyway. I can do the rest here."

Daniel considered the request a moment longer, although it was largely for effect. If a miracle of understanding stood to happen between people, the worst thing anyone could do would be to stand in the way of it.

"Just get some sleep. You don't need to stay up all night. If that pup stirs, you'll hear it."

Once Daniel had gone, the boys watched the pup for a while without saying anything, following the shallow rise and fall of its chest.

"How'd you know to bandage him up like that?" DJ asked finally.

"From a book."

"A book about dogs?" DJ asked.

Rodney smiled. "A book about the war. The Civil War. About a nurse who fixed up Union soldiers when they'd been shot."

DJ thought for a moment. "If it was me—I mean, just me—I'd have grabbed him and run quick as I could. That dog would probably be dead now. Bled to death on the way. You saved his life."

"He'd be dead if he was still down there in the creek bottom 'cause I wasn't strong enough to reach in and lift him out of there."

DJ turned to look at Rodney and, for the first time, he smiled. "I reckon it's a good thing we were both there. Took both of us to save him."

Rodney nodded, but as he watched the pup lying barely alive, his expression clouded. "He might still die. He was shot pretty bad."

Reaching over, DJ gently laid his hand on the pup's head and stroked it.

"He's our dog now," he said. "And we won't let him die."

Chapter Six

Earl Hammer

To look at his house was to know as much about Earl Hammer as anyone would care to know. Outside, the yard was overgrown with weeds. Rotting plywood lay strewn next to a rusting water heater that, in turn, leaned against an old refrigerator, its door yawning open, held by one hinge. Inside, the house was filled with old magazines, worn furniture and walls streaked with years of grime. The windows were so dirty that the place moldered in a state of perpetual twilight.

In the center of the kitchen stood a vinyl-covered card table with Earl seated at one side and Wylie at the other, his big frame teetering on the wobbly folding chair. Between them snaked a trail of dominoes.

"You realize what's happenin'?" Earl brayed, his voice thick with whiskey. "Right under your nose?"

"Shhh . . ." Wylie growled. "Don't have to yell at me." He tried to ignore Earl by staring intently at his dominoes, contemplating his next move, but to no avail.

"It's that son-in-law of yours. He's the problem. You just wait. He'll find a way to lose it all before you even know what hit ya."

"No one's gonna lose nuthin'." Wylie dismissed the notion with a snort.

"You think just because some boy married your daughter that makes him kin? Let me enlighten you 'bout family matters. There's two kinds of kin. There's blood kin. And then there's the kind he is. And I daresay no blood kin of mine would be inviting them colored into my house."

There was a knock on the door, and Earl turned unsteadily in the direction of the sound.

"Hello? Earl?" a muffled voice called from outside.

"Huh? What the hell?" Earl stumbled to his feet and lurched for the Remington propped against the wall before Wylie intercepted him.

"It's only Daniel," Wylie said. "Don't need to get all riled up every time someone knocks at the door."

"Daniel?" Earl stammered. "That you? Well, come on in here, Danny boy. Nobody in here 'ceptin' us chickens. Door's open. Come on in!"

Daniel pulled open the screen door and stepped into the room. It took a second for his eyes to adjust to the dim light, and his nose to the sour air.

"Evenin', Earl," he said, his voice polite but not overly friendly.

"Well, Danny boy, Danny boy . . . Let me get you a drink."

"No thanks, Earl. That's not why I came."

Earl raised his eyebrows in mock surprise. "Not why you came?" he said. "Then I don't suppose you come to play dominoes, now did ya?"

Daniel smiled. "Nope. Not that either. I came to talk."

"Talk?"

Daniel nodded.

"Well now," Earl said, "for you to interrupt your busy day jus' to talk, you must have something powerful important on your mind."

Daniel reached for one of the chairs and straddled it, resting his hands on top of the metal frame. "Earl," he began, "I don't much appreciate the idea of you goin' around shootin' dogs. Puppies, at that."

"Dogs?" Earl snapped. "Who said anything about shootin' dogs?"

"My boy and his pal found a puppy you shot and brought it back. They're trying to save it," Daniel replied, his voice calm and even.

Earl looked over at Wylie as if in disbelief. "That was a dog?" he said, shaking his head as if the very idea of shooting a dog was impossible. "I coulda sworn it was a coyote."

"It was only a pup. Mostly retriever I'd say, from the looks of 'im. Pretty hard to mistake for a coyote."

"Well, so what if'n it was? Somebody ought to shoot

every last one of them worthless strays. Ain't that right, Wylie?"

The old man looked up sharply. He had not wanted to be drawn into the discussion, and now Earl was asking him to take sides. His back stiffened.

Earl waited impatiently for Wylie to answer, his eyes on him hard and cold. Wylie tried to think what to say that would make Earl back off without seeming to condone what he'd done. Fortunately, Daniel saved him the trouble.

"Just 'cause a dog's unclaimed don't necessarily make 'im a stray, now does it? Besides that, those are my woods along the creek, not yours. I've never been one to accuse a neighbor of trespassing, and I ain't fixin' to do it now, but I would appreciate you being more careful. My kids play in there sometimes." He turned to his father-in-law. "Come on, Wylie. It's getting late. 'Night, Earl."

Wylie knew better than to argue, and he stiffly got to his feet. "You owe me thirty-five cents," he said to Earl.

"Thirty-five cents?" Earl snarled. He stood unsteadily in the middle of the room, never taking his eyes off Daniel.

"You boys can settle up later," Daniel said, clamping a hand on Wylie's shoulder as he steered him out the door.

They hadn't gone more than a few paces from the house before they heard the screen door fly open and slam shut.

Earl clung unsteadily to the porch rail with one hand and clutched the shotgun in the other. "I can shoot any stray I want!" he bellowed, his voice crackling with pure unbridled fury. "You hear me?" He lifted the shotgun to his shoulder and aimed it unsteadily at the two men. "Any goddamn stray I want!"

Daniel and Wylie didn't move. After a long minute, Earl lowered the Remington. Letting out a sigh of relief, Wylie ventured a step in his direction, holding his hands out at his sides, palms up. But the sight of Wylie walking toward him only seemed to rekindle Earl's fury, and he snapped the gun back to his shoulder.

"What business you got telling me what to do?" he sneered. "Cowardly, meddling folks like you." He cocked the hammer on the shotgun. "My boy's locked up on account of folks like you who can't leave well enough alone. And don't you think I don't know it."

"Earl," the old man said quietly, "put it down."

Earl shifted his aim from Wylie to Daniel and back again. Wylie paused for a moment before walking slowly toward the porch. The scene reminded Daniel of when he was a kid and his own father had taken him to Texarkana to see his first rodeo. More than anything he remembered the rodeo clowns when they would approach an angry Brahma bull, armed only with their wits. Watching Wylie approach Earl seemed a lot like that, only more dangerous.

"You set foot . . ." Earl bellowed again. "You set foot on this porch and I'll shoot you down. . . . I don't care who you are!"

Wylie shook his head. "No, you won't. You ain't shootin' nobody. Not till you pay up the thirty-five cents you owe me," he said.

Moving slowly, Wylie stepped onto the porch and didn't stop until the barrel of the Remington poked him squarely in the breastbone. Calmly he pushed the barrel aside and put his hand on Earl's shoulder and, leaning close, began to whisper in his ear.

Although Daniel couldn't make out anything Wylie was saying, the effect on Earl was immediate and profound, as if someone had punctured an old tire with an ice pick. Earl's shoulders began to soften and then shake, his head slumped forward and the shotgun slipped from his grasp, landing on the porch with a clatter.

The two men turned, arms around each other for support, and disappeared into the house. After several minutes the light in the window went dark and Wylie emerged and crossed to where Daniel had been waiting. Together, they turned for home.

"So?" Daniel asked. "He gonna be okay?"

"He's just bent up about his boy," Wylie said. "It's the whiskey talkin'. He don't mean nuthin' by it. Come morning, he'll likely have forgotten all about it. That's my guess."

"Well, morning's one thing. It's the rest of the night I worry about," Daniel said.

"Ah, he's harmless—just as long as he's by himself to sleep it off."

Daniel stopped suddenly. "So, tell me this. What happens when some night you're not around? What am I supposed to whisper in his ear to keep him from killing us all after one of his binges?"

Wylie shrugged.

"Just tell him he's being a fool. That's all I do. 'Earl,' I say, 'when your wife looks down from heaven and sees you, how do you think that makes her feel? Seeing you carry on like this?' I must have said it a hundred times."

"I'll have to remember that," Daniel said, but all the same, the thought didn't yield much comfort. "I just hope to heaven he don't up and shoot me before I get a chance to explain to him why he shouldn't."

"What about Lazarus?" Rodney volunteered.

"Lazarus!" DJ exclaimed. "What kind of name is Lazarus?"

The general commotion around the Burton breakfast table on most school mornings was such a time-honored tradition that Rodney's presence didn't seem all that unusual. Sarah was helping Bobby finish his oatmeal. Wylie was doing his best to scramble a clutch of eggs in an iron skillet while DJ and Rodney excitedly debated names for the pup.

"Lazarus came back from the dead," Rodney replied between bites of oatmeal topped high with brown sugar and butter.

"You can't name a dog Lazarus," DJ insisted. "Suppose you wanted to call him. Whatcha gonna yell? 'Here, Lazarus! Here, Lazarus!'"

"How 'bout Trigger," Sarah suggested, trying to be helpful as she mopped up the bowl of oatmeal that Bobby had spilled down the front of his pajamas.

"Trigger's a horse's name," DJ said, growing exasperated.

"You could name him Bullet," Wylie offered.

"That'd bring him running, given what he's been through," said Sarah.

"You might want to hold off on names for a little while," Daniel said, entering the kitchen. He had just come from the barn.

He looked up to see a table full of anxious faces looking back at him.

"He's not—?" DJ gasped.

"No, he's not," Daniel answered. "But he's not running around on all fours either. I'm just saying that, until we know, I'd hate to see you get all settled on a name and then find out he didn't make it."

"But he is doing better?" DJ asked.

"Well, at least he's no worse," Daniel said. Outside, Mr. Clancey sounded the opening toots of his daily recital on the bus horn. "There's the bus. Come on. You miss it and you're walking. Them's the rules."

"Them's the rules," repeated Bobby, his face covered with oatmeal.

"Ahh, now you got him doin' it," Wylie grumbled, "as if all your rules make any difference around here I can notice." No one had to remind him of the countless times DJ and Sarah had missed the bus and never once had to walk to school.

Sarah was first out the door, hoping to play shadowboard on the driveway, but to her surprise, the boys were fast on her heels, books and lunches in hand.

Suddenly DJ turned back.

"Check on him while we're gone," he said to his father, bursting through the door, out of breath. "Okay?"

"I will."

"See if he'll take some water," DJ added before disappearing and then, a second later, popping his head back in. "And try feedin' him. Maybe he'll eat something. I think he likes chicken."

Daniel followed him to the porch and waved. Out of habit, he turned to look over toward Earl Hammer's place, shading his eyes against the morning sun. It was usual, this hour of the morning, for Earl to be up, making his rounds, or at least for there to be smoke from the chimney. But this morning it was quiet on his side of the fence. He wondered if Wylie was right about Earl not remembering in the morning what had happened the night before. In a way he hoped so. Try as he might, there was something about the look in Earl's eyes Daniel couldn't forget. A hatred so consuming nothing could extinguish it.

✧ ✱ ✧

Rodney was the first on the bus and took his usual place in the back, where he could read without being bothered. Sarah was next, and she found her place among her busily chattering friends. But when DJ arrived he simply stood in the aisle.

"What's the matter, boy?" Mr. Clancey asked with obvious irritation in his voice. "Take your seat. We're late enough as it is."

If DJ heard him, it didn't make a difference. He remained standing in the aisle of the bus, pondering a great decision. He could see his friends, laughing and horsing around.

"What's the matter? You deaf, boy?" Mr. Clancey snapped, but still DJ hesitated.

Mr. Clancey turned in his driver's seat and gave DJ a shove. "Sit down!" he growled. "State regulations require every child to be seated, even if I have to seat you with the back of my hand. You understand, boy?"

DJ nodded.

"Well then?" Mr. Clancey demanded.

"Whatta you think of a dog named Lazarus?"

Mr. Clancey had to think for a second. "I think that's the silliest name for a dog I ever heard."

Again DJ nodded, this time thoughtfully. "Yeah," he said with a sigh. "That's what I thought. It just ain't gonna fly."

That settled, DJ headed down the aisle, past Sarah and her friends, past Jimmy Ray Thompson and Butch Waller, past the buffer zone and the other black children, who watched in silent amazement. He went all the way to the back of the bus, where he flopped down in the seat beside Rodney.

Surprised, Rodney looked up from his book. In fact, every face on the bus had turned around to stare in amazement at DJ. Even Mr. Clancey, forgetting how late he was, sat watching, his eyes glued to the wide rearview mirror.

"I thought we was late," DJ called out. "We ain't gettin' any earlier jus' sittin' here."

Mr. Clancey ground the bus noisily into gear and, slipping the clutch, headed down the road.

For a while the two boys rode along in silence.

"What if we call him Bandit?" DJ asked simply.

"Bandit?"

"Yeah. 'Cause he's an outlaw, like Jesse James, hunted down in cold blood. Nearly kilt."

Rodney thought for a second. "Bandit," he said again, trying the name on for size.

"Bandit the outlaw dog. Shot for stealin' chickens."

"That'll really make ol' Earl mad," Rodney said, snickering. "Every time he hears you call 'im, he'll think, 'That's the dog that ate my chickens.'"

"It's perfect," DJ concluded. "Bandit's the perfect name for 'im."

Daniel spent the morning trying to replace a rusted water pump on the old John Deere tractor, and it was nearly noon before he thought to look in on the pup. Approaching the stall, he stood near the door, watching.

The pup hadn't moved, and Daniel was sure for a moment it was dead. Quietly he knelt down in the fresh straw and gently stroked the pup.

It was still alive, breathing softly. Daniel felt the anger boil up in him again.

"How's he doin'?" Wylie asked, poking his head into the stall.

"Hasn't moved. Don't look too good, I'd say."

Wylie moved in closer to take a look for himself. "If I was you, I'd be mighty inclined to put him down yourself while the boy's at school. It's harder if he lingers."

Daniel considered for a second. "Probably right," he said. "But did you see how it brought them boys together?"

"Yeah," Wylie said. "I saw. But I can't imagine what good's gonna come outta that either."

"You know, Wylie, sometimes things seem to happen for a reason. I'm inclined to let this one just play itself out."

"Suit yourself," Wylie said, grimly looking over Daniel's shoulder at the stray. "But I think you're wasting your time."

As the bus shuddered to a stop at the Jerrit farm, this time both Rodney and DJ clambered down the stairwell and pounded on the doors. They practically flew up the long gravel driveway and didn't stop until they reached the barn.

The boys approached the stall and quietly peered in. What they saw made their hearts sink. The stall was empty.

Together they stood in shocked silence. Suddenly, as if the truth were too great to bear, DJ turned in his tracks and bolted for the door. Rodney could hear his footsteps echo through the dusty barn and the double doors slam hard behind him.

Alone and confused, Rodney debated what he should do. Head off after DJ? They had been friends only one day, and giving chase seemed a little risky. Perhaps it was best to stay put. But as he waited, alone in the empty stall, he couldn't bring himself to believe the pup was gone. They had been so careful carrying him to the barn. They had cleaned the wound and bandaged it and had stayed all night just to keep him company. For him to have died was almost more than Rodney could take. He felt his knees weaken, and it seemed easier just to slump down in the straw. He closed his eyes to try to block out the sadness.

As he knelt there, he was suddenly aware of the strangest sensation.

Something was licking his hand.

Peering under the feed trough, he saw a pair of eyes looking back at him. At first he couldn't believe it.

"Bandit?" he whispered. "Bandit?"

In response, the pup whimpered. Rodney held out his hand, and again Bandit licked it with his warm soft tongue.

In the time it took to realize it wasn't a dream, Rodney jumped from the straw and headed around the corner of the stall on a dead run, nearly colliding with Wylie.

"It's Bandit!" Rodney announced in a voice so loud it startled a pair of crows in the top of the barn, setting them flapping and cawing loudly. "It's Bandit! He's alive!" He rushed past Wylie, through the barn doors, following the same path DJ had taken moments before.

"DJ!" his voice rang out. "It's Bandit! He's alive! Bandit's alive!"

Wylie watched him go, irritated as always at any

commotion, but it took only a moment before his curiosity got the better of him.

At first he saw nothing.

"That boy's possessed," he muttered. Nevertheless he struggled down to his knees to look under the feed trough, the one place where something could possibly hide, and came eye to eye with the pup, who rewarded his efforts by licking the old man on the nose.

"Well, I'll be switched," he grumbled, almost disappointed that his dire predictions had missed by such a wide mark. "I wouldn't have given you a chance in a hundred," he told the dog. "Not even one in a thousand."

Unimpressed by the odds, Bandit licked the old man again on the nose. For once, Wylie didn't seem to mind.

Book Two
Friends

Chapter One

The Discovery

Whatta we need to get?" DJ asked as the boys approached the ramshackle building that looked more like it belonged to a pack rat than the most influential black man in all of Canaan. The official name of the place was Emmanuel Shoup's Mercantile and Supply, but all the people like Miss Eunice who lived on the outskirts of Canaan knew it simply as "Shoup's."

"Dark molasses and something else." Rodney dug into his shirt pocket for the list Miss Eunice had written out for him in big scrolly letters. "Dark molasses and Clabber Girl."

"Can't forget the Clabber Girl," DJ added, not willing to admit that he had no idea what Clabber Girl was.

In the time since he and Rodney had rescued Bandit, the two had become best friends. They had both just turned fifteen. DJ was ruggedly built like Daniel, getting broad in the shoulders and tanned, his hair so blond from the sun it was nearly white. By contrast, Rodney was lean, his features more finely cast.

All the while, the world beyond Canaan was changing, too. Americans cheered as John Glenn orbited the earth and listened with stunned disbelief at the tragic news out of Dallas that President Kennedy had been shot. Even now, all over America, boys not much older than DJ and Rodney were saying good-bye to their families and packing their bags for a faraway place called Vietnam. Not that events of even that magnitude did much to change ordinary life in the piney thickets of eastern Texas. Only weather and prices could do that.

DJ turned and whistled. "Come on, Bandit!" He watched as a handsome dog with a dark brown shiny coat and white markings around his throat like a bandanna bounded out of the bushes and headed for the two boys. Bandit, too, had grown strong and healthy. He sniffed the air and trotted stiffly off in the direction of the Mercantile. "Reckon he's got a sniffer on ol' Shoup's pork rinds," DJ said.

"Now watch when we get in there." Rodney's voice was low and conspiratorial. "Shoup'll be somewhere in the back, so he'll send out LeRoy. And LeRoy won't be able to find anything. Especially the Clabber Girl. He'll look and he'll look and he'll look some more." Rodney acted it out, stretching and peering around as if looking for something far more serious than a can of baking powder. "Then, from the back, ol' man Shoup'll boom out in that voice of his, 'LeRoy? What you lookin' fo'?' But LeRoy, rather than admit to his daddy that he can't find it, he'll just ignore him and say to us, all serious as can be, 'I think we outta that Clabber Girl.'"

Rodney clamped a hand on DJ's shoulder, bringing him in close. "An' then from the back, ol' Shoup'll say, 'Whatta we outta?'" he boomed into DJ's ear, "and he'll come storming out like thunder." Rodney strutted just like he pictured Shoup would strut, while DJ held one hand over his ringing ear and the other on his side, which was beginning to ache from laughing so hard. Rodney did the voices perfectly, playing each character just right—the expression on ol' Shoup as he raised his eyebrows and glared down at LeRoy, and then LeRoy's face as he cowered up at his father. It was perfect.

"What happens then?" DJ gasped, working hard to catch his breath.

"Well, the way I see it, Shoup'll come over to us and look us in the eye like we had created some kind of horrible nuisance for everyone, an' he'll say, 'Whatta you boys lookin' fo' that's so troublesome to find?' And I'll just reach over and pick up a can of Clabber Girl, right where LeRoy's been lookin' for ten minutes, an' I'll say, 'Why, Mr. Shoup, I've jus' been lookin' fo' this.'"

It was several minutes before the boys had composed themselves enough to not burst out laughing whenever they so much as looked at each other. Gamely they put on their serious faces and pushed through the torn screen door, two boys on a serious mission.

Shoup's was crammed with things. Mason jars for canning. Tools for everything from fence mending to well digging. There were large bags of feed and rolls of copper pipe. Running down the center of the store like a spine was a set of shelves with canned goods, some of them with labels so dusty they might have dated back to the time when Texas was a republic. It seemed impossible that so small a store could hold so much.

Emmanuel Shoup's youngest boy, LeRoy, was so busy trying to hit a big blue buzzer fly with a rolled-up newspaper, he scarcely noticed as the boys entered the store. Rodney picked out the molasses right away and then, giving a little look to DJ as if to say "watch this," he began to pace slowly in front of the shelves, looking high and low with labored, studious concentration. It was a studied performance and DJ settled back against the wall to enjoy the show.

It took LeRoy a while to even notice. The fly was proving to be a worthy, not to mention durable, adversary. It had withstood a flurry of near misses and even a couple of direct hits before it sputtered wildly, ricocheting off the Orange Crush sign in an obvious death spiral and plummeted behind the bottles of milk of magnesia. LeRoy allowed himself a moment to savor his victory before looking up.

"Help you find sumptin'?" he asked, jamming the newspaper into his back pocket to keep it handy.

"Miss Eunice needs some Clabber Girl," Rodney said.

LeRoy stopped and considered, rubbing his chin as if the whole situation required a great deal of thought. "Clabber Girl . . . Clabber Girl . . . Let's see now. . . ." With great deliberation, LeRoy scanned the shelves, peering intently at each label, searching high and low, and each time managing to somehow peer his way right past the stack of cans where the Clabber Girl, holding her plate of biscuits, smiled slyly back. Finally, with obvious disgust, LeRoy shook his head, as if the whole secret of life had somehow eluded him.

"I reckon we out of Clabber Girl," LeRoy said.

From the back of the cluttered shop, as if on cue, a voice boomed. "Whatta we out of?" A moment later, Emmanuel Shoup himself arrived, out of breath and thoroughly bothered by the very notion that he would be out of anything a soul would find itself in need of. "What you boys lookin' fo' that's so hard to find?"

"LeRoy says you're fresh out," Rodney said.

"Fresh out? Fresh out of what?" Shoup boomed again.

"I reckon fresh out of this," Rodney said calmly as he reached out directly in front of him and picked a can of Clabber Girl off the shelf.

The successful finding of the item in question, far from being a cause for celebration, only made Shoup madder. "You spent this whole time lookin' for that? Why didn't you say so? We ain't never outta that."

He turned to LeRoy.

"What's the matter with you, boy?" Shoup roared. "I got me two whole cases of Clabber Girl in the back. Why, you're the one that put these here out on the shelves jus' yesterday. So why you tellin' these boys we outta Clabber Girl? You ain't got the common sense the Good Lord Almighty gave a duck! You got anything to say for yourself, boy? Anything?"

LeRoy peered around the bags of goat chow. "I kilt

that fly you told me to kill," he said. "I kilt it deader 'n dead."

From beneath the sanctuary of the row of milk of magnesia, the fly bestirred itself and, with a stumbling blue buzz, completed one last sweeping arc before crashing in infamy into Shoup's ample nose.

DJ was still laughing when the two boys turned onto the driveway that led up to Miss Eunice's house. "The look on his face," DJ said, raising his eyebrows until they almost jumped off his forehead, "and then the fly. LeRoy's sayin' 'I kilt it dead' just in time to have it dive-bomb ol' Shoup in the snozzola." DJ thought for a second. "So, how'd you know what everybody was gonna say?"

"Just a game I play," answered Rodney.

"A game?"

"It's like a listening game. Most people just hear enough to understand. They don't really listen. You listen good enough to what someone is saying and pretty soon you'll know what they're gonna say next even before they say it."

"That's—"

"A buncha baloney?" Rodney interrupted. "See? I knew you were gonna say that."

"Now talk about—"

"A pucky pile?" Rodney interrupted again. "You're sure makin' this easy."

"You're just guessin' lucky," DJ muttered. "If I was to say something original, you wouldn't have any idea what I was saying."

"If you was to say something original, neither one of us would have any idea what you were saying," Rodney said, giving his friend a good-natured little shove in the back.

A wonderful aroma was coming from Miss Eunice's kitchen. The boys peered around the corner to investigate. A kettle of stew was simmering on the stove, the lid giving an occasional rattle. Off to the side of the oven, on the shelves Miss Eunice called her "risin' shelves," bread dough in mixing bowls was already nudging up against damp towels and filling the kitchen with the friendly smells of freshly ground wheat flour and yeast. Two greased and floured bread pans stood ready for the dough once it had been kneaded a final time and shaped into loaves.

"Grandma?" Rodney called, but there was no answer.

"She's probably out weedin' the tobacco patch," DJ said. It was the name he had given to Miss Eunice's garden.

Together they headed out of the kitchen, letting the screen door slam behind them, down the path to the garden.

"You take beans and peas. I'll take greens and turnips."

"Who's got watermelons?" DJ asked.

"Whoever gets there first."

DJ turned at the first row of pole beans, some of them grown so high they were nearly overhead. Across the garden, he could hear Rodney calling. "Grandma?! DJ's here! He wants to help with pickin' tobacco!"

DJ laughed. So much had changed since that first time in the garden.

"Miss Eunice?" DJ called. "Rodney couldn't catch any lake perch, so he brought you a nice, ripe skunk." From across the garden, he heard Rodney laugh. Then something caught his eye and he stopped.

"Miss Eunice?" he said, his voice low, almost a whisper.

She lay on the ground, peacefully, as if she had decided to curl up for a nap. Beside her, a basket half full of runner beans lay tipped on its side, the other half scattered on the ground. DJ knelt down beside her and gently touched her cheek with his hand.

"Rodney," he said, so softly it was barely even spoken at all. Then louder, "Rodney! Rodney, I found her."

The quaver in his voice said all that needed saying.

The music arrived in waves. Great voices, rich and full of sorrow, tugged and pulled at one another in little eddies and currents before swelling together. The choir, dressed in white robes with red satin trim, swayed gently to the music, feeling the power of the old hymn as it welled up inside. When it was the women's turn for a verse, their voices rose to the portals of heaven in praise and sorrow, filling the small Baptist church with sound.

Safe in the arms of Jesus,
    safe from corroding care,
Safe from the world's temptations,
    sin cannot harm me there.

And then it was the men's turn, their voices deep and resonant, solid as the warm Texas earth.

Free from the blight of sorrow,
    free from my doubts and fears;
Only a few more trials,
    only a few more tears!

In the congregation, some breathed the words silently, knowing the verses by heart; others listened with closed eyes, tears finding their way down weathered faces. All had known Miss Eunice and all loved her.

On the rostrum, his back to the choir, Reverend Cecil Robbins sat with closed eyes, drawing inspiration from the music. For thirty years he had pastored the Faithful Missionary Baptist Church and had been present at the births and deaths, the illnesses and accidents, the triumphs and the tragedies of his flock, offering comfort when he could, but always careful to remind everyone that the only true comfort came from the Lord.

Directly in front of the minister rested a simple box of white pine. On either side of the box were floral sprays of gladiolus and iris, and draped over the top was the old story quilt, folded to reveal the happier scenes—the abundant harvest and the young black girl with the colorful pigtails.

Now the congregation joined in, uninvited but welcome. Some took to their feet, pressing forward, surrounding the front pew, the mourners' bench where Rodney and DJ sat, engulfing them with their love and sympathy.

Near the back, surrounded by dark faces, the other members of the Burton family sat together. Only Wylie was absent. As all the voices joined for the final verse, Bobby craned his neck one last time, straining to see through the forest of people standing in the back if Grandpa had changed his mind and come.

Safe in the arms of Jesus,
  safe on His gentle breast
There by His love o'ershaded,
  sweetly my soul shall rest.

For what seemed a full minute, the sound reverberated through the small church and gradually fell away until there was nothing left but the whisper of paper fans and the muffled sounds of grief.

Slowly, Reverend Robbins rose and crossed to the casket. He looked into the expectant faces in the congregation.

"Safe in the arms of Jesus," he began, his voice low and tender. "Our beloved Sister Eunice is, even now, safe in the arms of Jesus. At rest from the trials of this life. The cares of this life. The heartache of this life."

"A life free from tribulation?" he called out. There was a murmur from the congregation. "Oh, no. There was much tribulation. A husband taken early. In the very prime of life. Leaving her alone with a daughter to raise. Yes, there was tribulation!"

Yes, yes, the congregation sighed.

"And this same daughter she had to raise by her own hand, this daughter who herself tragically fell to the snares of Babylon, leaving a young boy to raise in the pathway of righteousness! Oh, yes, there was always tribulation!"

Yes, yes. There was tribulation. There was always tribulation, they murmured as those near the mourners' bench pressed even closer to Rodney.

"It was not an *easy* life for Sister Eunice. It was not a *painless* life for Sister Eunice." He stopped, looking down at the two boys, who looked back up at him, their eyes expectant. Reverend Robbins lowered his voice, held out his arms as if to gather in a stray lamb. "Not an easy life. But it was a *faithful* life." He lifted his voice to the rafters. "Do you believe in the glory, in the majesty of one faithful life?"

Yes, yes! Praise Jesus! The congregation was on its feet, again pressing forward to surround the mourners' bench. Robbins waited for the wave of emotion to ebb and the cries to settle before looking out over the congregation, his gaze landing on the Burtons.

"And who is there among us today, at this dark and troubling hour, who wouldn't trade *all* earthly glory to be gently rocked—for all eternity!—safe in the blessed arms of Jesus. Let us pray."

As the sea of heads bowed and those closest to the mourners' bench reached their hands and placed them on the backs and heads of the two boys, Reverend Robbins offered up to heaven a stirring prayer for the soul of Miss Eunice Freeman. This time, neither Rodney nor DJ peeked.

Chapter Two

The Choice

Rodney sat quietly on the top step of the small kitchen porch. He had worked since daybreak to put the house in order. Miss Eunice's things had been sifted and sorted before being tucked neatly into boxes and stacked in the closet. The bedding had been folded, the kitchen cleaned, the pots and pans scoured and the floor swept.

In the hours and days following Miss Eunice's death, there had been an outpouring of concern for the boy. Aunt Celie had begged him to move in with her and her three young children, as had Reverend Robbins and his wife and a handful of relatives, neighbors and friends. They had all expressed their loving concern, and he had thanked each of them for their kindness.

"I'll decide when I'm ready," he said simply. "I need some time to settle things."

That morning he had begun to pack, and by noon all his things sat forlornly in the middle of his bedroom. The books, even the torn halves of *The Deerslayer*, had been packed into boxes. So had his shirts and trousers and Sunday suit, which rested neatly on top. Books, clothes and a few of Miss Eunice's important papers for safekeeping—that was all there was that seemed worth taking.

As he sat on the porch, he wondered again if he could ever really leave. The memories of growing up in that house were powerful. The aromas of fresh bread baking, savory stews simmering all day in the big kettle, bacon and corn fritters sizzling in the frying pan on a cold morning were a part of that house. He remembered summers with the tart sweetness of apricots and peaches being cooked down into jam, and autumns with the smell of turkey and sausage dressing on Thanksgiving morning.

Out front, the familiar rattle of the Burtons' truck interrupted the quiet morning as it pulled to a stop in front of the house. Rodney heard the front screen open and slam shut and listened as the footsteps echoed through the house, pausing in the hallway outside his bedroom. He heard DJ's disgusted little snort.

"Shoulda known he'd be wantin' to move the whole United States Library of Congress," DJ yelled from the bedroom. Rodney only smiled. "Hey, boy, where you at?" DJ poked his head out the kitchen door. "There you are. Well? It's been a week. You coming or not?"

It wasn't until that very moment Rodney knew for sure.

"It's got nuthin' to do with that boy," Wylie said, his voice sharp with anger. For most of the morning Daniel had been cleaning out the utility shed, which stood next to the house. Wylie had watched him in silence, glowering each time he passed, but when Daniel started cutting up perfectly good sheets of plywood and hammering them up to make walls, Wylie knew the whole notion had gone

121

way too far. He simply had no choice but to speak his mind.

"Okay," Daniel said. "Then what's it got to do with, Wylie?" He paused to trim one edge with a Skilsaw.

"It's got to do with economics. Prices are the lowest in five years. Even if we did have enough to sell, we don't get nuthin' for it. What with the frost and the drought, I don't know where they're getting enough yield to drive them prices down, but it sure ain't in Canaan, Texas. We'll be lucky to feed the mouths we've got."

Daniel held the plywood in place and, with practiced strokes, quickly nailed it to the studs before taking a step back to admire his work. He wasn't a finish carpenter by anyone's definition but all in all it wasn't bad. "We'll get by," he said, unbuckling his tool belt. "We always have."

"I don't know where you got it in your head that it's our job to take in every stray and orphan that comes along. He's got kin. Let his own folk take him in," Wylie said, the red flush of anger beginning to creep up his neck. "Our duty is to our own and *only* our own. That's the simple truth of it and you know it."

Daniel didn't answer right away. "Rodney ain't 'every stray or orphan' now, is he? Besides, where else is he gonna go? A boy his age shouldn't be living alone out there. It ain't right. And all the work he's done with DJ getting his grades up and getting him reading, he's practically part of the family already."

Daniel ran his hand over the walls, tapping a little here and there with the handle of the hammer to smooth out the seams. He'd bring power over from the house in a day or two so there'd be lights and the boy could use a kerosene heater when the weather turned cold. It would work fine for a bunkhouse.

"Let me tell you something about family," Wylie said. "There's family. And then there's *blood* family. You confuse the two and there's always trouble. Earl's not gonna like this one bit, having that boy moving in. And Earl's not alone."

Daniel gave the room one last look and, with a self-satisfied little nod, closed the door behind him.

"So," he said, draping an arm over Wylie's shoulder, "here's a question for ya: If ol' Earl Hammer's got so much to say, what I want to know is, who you plannin' on answering to come the Judgment Day? The Good Lord? Or Earl Hammer?"

There was little Wylie Jerrit hated more than being wrong, but for all his apprehension and grumbling, he had to admit having Rodney on the farm was turning out to be much more of a blessing than a curse. They could always use the extra hand, and any fool could see how hardworking the boy was. Plus, unlike DJ, he cheerfully did what he was told and generally stayed far enough out of sight that even Earl could have missed the fact that he was living there. What's more, even Wylie was beginning to suspect that this boy was blessed with much more than just a pleasant nature and a strong back; he had a gift.

Each night, long after the dishes had been cleared and all that remained of the freshly baked apple cobbler was a few crumbs on the bottom of the pan, the family clustered around the table, stubbornly refusing to leave, waiting for Rodney to tell a story.

Daniel would lean back in his chair and rest his eyes, while Bobby sat upright, *his* eyes eager and wide. Wylie, keeping order at the head of the table, would pack his pipe with Black Castle and begin filling the air with lazy clouds of smoke, trying hard to appear bored but fooling no one.

Every night DJ would pose a familiar question.

"So what was your uncle's name again?"

"Who?"

"Your uncle. The one on the train?"

"Oh, him? Well, his name was Sylvester Dolf Freeman, but everyone just called him Uncle Porky." Rodney would smile and the others would settle in, hanging on every detail.

"Uncle Porky was a Pullman conductor on the Twentieth Century Limited, which ran from New York to Chicago. The most beautiful train in the world. But by the time I was little, he had retired, which meant he spent all day just being underfoot, and finally my Aunt

Elva got word to Miss Eunice that she wanted her to come up and visit, especially since Porky had taken to having spells."

"Spells? What's a spell?" Bobby asked.

"That's an old-fashioned word for when someone old starts actin' funny," Sarah explained.

"Like Grandpa?" Bobby asked as all the others roared in laughter—all except, of course, Wylie.

"You won't think it's so funny when I double your chores," Wylie answered.

"Sounds pretty funny to me," DJ said.

"Finish your story," Daniel said, his eyes still closed, sounding a little like a judge ordering a reluctant witness to testify.

"Well," Rodney continued, "Miss Eunice agreed, and bright and early one June morning we went up to visit. Now at first, everything seems pretty much as it should. At least until it's time for bed. Now, we're fast asleep. Middle of the night. And all of a sudden the door flies open and there's Porky standing there, wearing nuthin' but his conductor's hat, yelling 'All Aboard! Booooard!'

Scared me half out of my wits."

"He was nekked?" Bobby asked.

"Nekked front and center," Rodney answered. "Now Miss Eunice, she rises straight up in bed and looks at Porky standing there without a stitch and, calm as can be, she announces, 'I beg your pardon, Mr. Conductor, but this ain't our train. We're on the five fifteen.' He just nodded, tipped his cap and closed the door. I guess Aunt Elva had warned her he might do something, but nobody bothered to tell me."

Daniel leaned back even farther in his chair and smiled while DJ buried his face in the crook of his elbow and slapped the table with his hand. Wylie simply shook his head and laughed a deep, raspy wheeze that sounded like coarse sandpaper on old wood. Only Bobby sat transfixed, reflecting on what must have seemed a glimpse into one of life's more profound mysteries.

"What happened then?" Bobby gasped.

"Well, what happened then was Miss Eunice got herself dressed, and together she and Elva went out after him. He was outside by then, workin' his way down the street, when they finally caught up to him. Wearing just his hat. Now, Uncle Porky, there was a man who knew conductorin'."

Another wave of laughter washed over the table, and when it passed, everyone fell silent.

"I hope you're writing these down," Sarah said finally.

"Writing what down?" Rodney asked, a little surprised at the notion.

"These stories. You need to write your stories down."

"Aw, they're just stories," Rodney said. "Everybody's got stories."

"Not like yours," Bobby piped. "You tell stories better'n anyone in the whole world. Twice as better."

Rodney smiled. "Lots of good storytellers in the whole world, Bobber. Someday, when you're older, you curl yourself up with a book like *The Adventures of Huckleberry Finn* and then we'll talk about who's the best storyteller in the whole world."

"Still, Sarah's right," Daniel said. "You should be writing yours down. Time has a way of stealin' 'em. It's too easy to forget things, no matter how hard you try to remember." There was a hint of regret in his voice.

Rodney considered the idea for a moment and then smiled. "Maybe I will someday," he said. "You never can tell."

The harvest sun beat down, sending shimmering heat in waves across the land and making everyone feel thick and slow and lazy. Daniel and the boys were working to harvest feed corn. As Daniel drove the old International Harvester, the boys followed behind, gleaning what the machinery had missed. In good years, they might have left a little behind for the birds to forage, but this hadn't been a good year. The yield was down and leaving even one ear of corn in the field seemed a luxury no one could afford.

By midday the work had gotten chokingly hot, and the boys were glad when lunchtime came. It was a chance to cool down, stretch out and enjoy the quiet without the roar of blades and gears and the clouds of chaff that made it almost impossible to breathe.

The boys devoured the lunch Sarah had packed—

meatloaf sandwiches and cherry pie. They leaned back against the harvester, finding what shade they could. Not far away, Daniel was stretched out on a tarp, his sweat-soaked hat pulled low over his face.

"Hey, DJ?" Rodney asked. It was a second or two before the reply came back, as if the sound had taken that long to travel in the afternoon heat.

"Hmmm?"

"Can I ask you something?"

"Sure," DJ replied. "Ask me whatever you want."

Rodney thought for a moment. "How old were you when your mama died?"

"She died when I was six," DJ answered. "Why you wanna know that?"

"Just wondering, that's all."

DJ grunted, his way of saying it was reason enough. A minute or two passed before Rodney asked again.

"You remember her much?"

"My mama?"

"Yeah."

DJ sighed. "For one thing, she's the reason we ain't got a TV."

"Why? What's she got to do with the TV?"

"Dad was fixin' to get one the second they come out, but she said, 'Nuthin' good'll ever came out of a thing with so many buttons on it.' I reckon he feels it wouldn't be right to get one now."

Rodney smiled. "I thought you did it just to get Wylie out of the house. Give him a reason to go down to Earl's so he could watch the fights." He tugged on a piece of grass, bit the end of it, wrinkled his nose and spit it back out. "What else you remember?"

"I remember how she looked. Her face. At least I think I do. Some of that is from pictures I've seen of her. After a while it's hard to know what you really remember from when she was alive and what you remember from the pictures."

There followed a long silence. Overhead, a hawk made lazy figure eights above the newly harvested fields, looking for mice that might have gotten distracted by the commotion and become easy prey.

"How 'bout yours?" DJ asked finally. "You remember your mama?"

Rodney shook his head. "I was a baby when she left."

"Why you figure she done it? You ever ask Miss Eunice?"

"Miss Eunice said my mama was like a wild wind the devil himself couldn't tame."

DJ propped himself up on one elbow and looked out over the fields, trying to imagine Rodney's mother whirling across the countryside like a tornado with the devil in hot pursuit.

"She didn't keep no photographs? Miss Eunice, I mean? Just so you could know what your mama looked like?"

Rodney shook his head again. "Miss Eunice said the less I saw the less I'd wanna know, and the less I knew the better."

DJ grunted in agreement. "If I knew any less about anything, I'd be darn near perfect." He lazily tossed a stone in the direction of the harvester, but it didn't even make it halfway.

"But she did write me a letter." Rodney smiled to himself, and hearing it in his voice, DJ looked over.

"Who did?"

"My mama."

"She did? When?"

"You know the day we moved my things? I was going through some of Miss Eunice's papers, and there was a letter addressed to me. My mama sent it ten years ago."

"How come Miss Eunice never gave it to you?"

"I reckon she thought it would upset me."

"Well? Did it?" DJ asked.

"It just said that she left because it was best and not to blame Miss Eunice for sending her away."

"That's all? That ain't much for someone so long gone." DJ was obviously disappointed. He had hoped for something more scandalous from a wild woman the devil himself couldn't tame.

Rodney took his time before answering. On the

ground beside him an ant struggled to move a parched kernel of corn many times its size, first pushing determinedly from one side before turning to tug furiously from the other. Reaching down he moved a small twig out of its path. Why should everyone have so hard a harvest?

"She said that she had never stopped thinking about me, every day of her life, from sunup till past dark, and that she always would, no matter if she ever saw me again." Rodney shrugged. "I guess Miss Eunice saw no comfort in me knowing that."

DJ grunted his agreement. "Think you'd recognize her if you ever saw her all grown up?"

"Dunno," Rodney answered. "Maybe if I saw something of myself in her."

Again DJ grunted. "Wouldn't count on it."

"Count on what?"

"Seeing much of yourself in her."

"Why not?"

DJ let out a low chuckle. "I jus' doubt your mama could possibly be sufficient ugly to look very much like *you*. That's all."

Rodney leveled a look of cold disdain at his friend. "I'll show you ugly," he said, suddenly pouncing on DJ and sending both of them sprawling and laughing onto the warm stubble.

The commotion roused Daniel enough to pop an eye out from under the brim of his hat. "You two ain't learned a thing," he said, propping himself up on one elbow to watch. "That's what started all this in the first place—you two calling each other names."

Crossing to the boys, he picked up each one by an arm and good-naturedly shoved them in the direction of the harvester.

"All right, now. Back to work," he called over his shoulder as he climbed into the seat of the harvester and started it up. "What's gonna be ugly is if we don't finish this before dark!"

Still laughing and shoving, the boys grudgingly fell in line behind the harvester, picking up the widows and orphans and tossing them into the hopper, trying hard not to miss a single one.

✧ ✳ ✧

Daniel and DJ waited their turn at the grain elevator as the foreman weighed and reweighed the trucks that arrived, their beds filled with ripe ears of seed corn or hopped full with mounds of yellow milo. The other farmers came and went, stopping only briefly to talk, taking some comfort in the fact that it had been a tough year for everybody.

When it was Daniel's turn, the foreman frowned as he checked the scale and jotted down some numbers on a bright orange weight ticket.

"That the last of it?" he asked.

Daniel nodded. "Hardly worth my trouble even bringing it in."

"Don't feel too bad." The foreman tried to sound cheerful. "You got lots of company this year, what with the prices being so soft. Let's hope it's better next year."

"It better be," Daniel said. "If not it's likely I'll just plow it under . . . before it plows me."

They rode home in silence. It was only after Daniel pulled the truck to a stop in front of the house that DJ found the courage to ask the question that had been buzzing in his head since they left the grain elevator.

"Dad?" he asked. "How bad is it?"

Daniel tugged on the bill of DJ's cap. "Don't you go worryin'," he said.

"But what if next year's as bad as this? Are we gonna lose the farm?"

"There'll always be bad years. We've just had a string of 'em, that's all. But we'll get by. We always do. Now best get washed up for supper. I'll be in directly."

As DJ pushed open the front door, he was met with the warm aroma of supper cooking. Sarah poked her head out of the kitchen, her hands covered with biscuit dough.

"If you're going out back, tell 'em supper's on in fifteen minutes so they need to wash up."

Behind the house, Bobby was teaching Rodney to pitch horseshoes. As Rodney waited his turn, Bobby confidently tossed two leaners followed by a ringer that landed with a resounding metal *clank*. DJ tried not to laugh as Rodney's final toss skipped awkwardly and rolled nearly all the way to the barn.

"That's points," Rodney claimed.

"Is not," Bobby insisted.

"Why not? Look how far it went! It's gotta be worth something."

DJ put his fingers to his mouth and whistled. "Sarah says wash up," he called. "Supper's on."

"Hey, DJ?" Rodney called back. "Don'tcha get points for throwin' the farthest?"

"Only in hand grenades, not horseshoes."

"See?" Bobby argued. "'Sides, that wasn't throwin', that was rollin'."

DJ watched as they trudged, laughing and arguing, toward the barn to collect the errant horseshoe. Beyond them, the fields looked like velvet in the twilight, the stubble soft and golden from a distance, rimmed by the darkening blue sky. For a moment, it didn't even matter how bad the harvest had been.

Chapter Three

The Wrinkle Pine

Each morning for a week, DJ had kept a weather eye, hoping that Saturday morning would dawn bright. For days the skies had remained a cold leaden gray and there had been periods of rain and sleet. Now, even before the eastern sky was much more than the faintest rosy pink, he knew he had gotten his wish. Excitedly he made the rounds, first to where Bobby slept, nudging him awake, and then out the back door and around the side of the house to Rodney's room.

"Wake up," he said, poking him in the ribs. "Rodney, wake up. It's time."

"Time for what?" Rodney asked, still mostly asleep.

"Time to find a wrinkle pine."

"Why do you want a wrinkle pine? Why not get a straight one?"

"You'll have to ask Bobber," DJ said.

Like reluctant recruits they assembled outside the tool shed, sleepy and shivering against the cold, as DJ removed from the Peg-Board the things they'd need: a long-handled axe, a tape measure, a ragged coil of manila rope. "Whatta we missin'?" he asked.

"Don't ask me. I never did this before." Rodney yawned.

"You and Miss Eunice never went hunting for a wrinkle pine?" Bobby asked, surprised.

"About the only time Miss Eunice went looking for a tree was when she decided to cut herself a new hickory switch."

Outside the tool shed, Bandit was barking, eager for an adventure in the woods.

"Come on!" Bobby urged impatiently. "Bandit's ready to go."

"Hold your horses," DJ said. "You wanna cut it down with your bare hands?"

Carefully he stacked the tools and rope in the wheelbarrow, and they headed off toward the rolling hills south of the farm. Bandit led the way, barking and chasing down any rabbit brave enough to stick out its nose on so cold a December morning.

As Bobby ran ahead, DJ and Rodney walked easily along together, enjoying the morning and each other's company.

"So, you're tellin' me that Miss Eunice used to switch you pretty good? Sweet ol' woman like that?"

"Sweet ol' woman?" Rodney snorted. "It was the wrath of God if'n she caught you lyin'. She may have been small, but if she found herself the right switch, with just enough flex in it, she could make plain the error of your ways quicker than you could beg for forgiveness."

"Maybe that explains how come you turned out like you did," DJ observed.

"Yeah," Rodney said. "I reckon it explains a lot of things. Like why I'm scared to go into the woods."

The image of Miss Eunice sternly approaching, switch in hand like an avenging angel, was so vivid that DJ tripped over the wheelbarrow, spilling the coil of rope and half the tools out on the ground. Without a word, Rodney helped him pick the things up, a little smile showing at the corners of his mouth. He liked that he could make DJ laugh, surprise him with something that seemed serious at first but was really a joke—and it would take DJ a second to figure it out before he would throw his head back and roar with laughter.

"Well," DJ said, "don't worry. If I spot a hickory tree that looks menacing, I'll protect ya."

Up ahead, Bandit was off and running, and Bobby, tired of trying to keep up with him, fell back with the others as they hiked along through the stands of scrub pine.

"DJ?" Bobby asked excitedly. "When we find a wrinkle pine, can I chop it down?"

"Nope. Axes are for big kids. Your job is to be the scout and find the perfect one."

"How do we know if it's perfect?" Bobby asked.

"I don't know. You just look at it and if something inside tells you it's the perfect one, it probably is."

"Your brother's a philosopher," Rodney said, turning to Bobby. "He said what Plato would say, except that what you're actually seeing is only a representation of the perfect tree. He called this world the cave of shadows."

"I know where there are some caves!" Bobby said excitedly. "Wanna see? Come on!" With renewed energy he charged off, disappearing behind a small ridgeline.

DJ threw a weary look at Rodney. "Now see what you've done?" he muttered. "He's gonna think trees grow in caves."

They hadn't walked more than fifty paces when suddenly they heard a shout. "I found it! I found it!" Bobby yelled. "I found a wrinkle pine!"

The tree was magnificent, full and symmetrical. Its branches were evenly spaced, and the needles were shorter and greener than those of all the other scrub pines. Rodney took one look at it and immediately he understood.

"You meant a *regal* pine," he said.

"That's what I said," replied Bobby with Bandit

nipping at his heels. "A wrinkle pine."

DJ shrugged. "It's what my dad always called 'em when he was a kid."

"I didn't know they even grew around here."

"They don't. Not very many of 'em, anyway. You have to know where to look." DJ turned to Bobby. "So, Bobber, you sure this is the one? Think it'll fit?"

DJ reached into the wheelbarrow and tossed him the tape measure. "Better be sure. No sense hauling it all the way back if it won't fit."

"I know it'll fit," Bobby said. "It's just gotta."

As Bobby pointed and Bandit barked, Rodney took his aim, tapping the axe blade cautiously against the trunk. Then he swung with all his strength. And again and again until, just when he thought his arms would drop, from somewhere deep in the heartwood came a crackle, One. Two. Three more strokes and the regal pine was theirs.

Not surprisingly, the trip back was much slower going, with Rodney and DJ taking turns pushing the wheelbarrow, while Bobby steadied the tree as it bumped along over the ridges and gullies.

By the time the boys got back it was well after breakfast and they were tired and hungry. Sarah watched skeptically as they maneuvered the tree toward the door and shook her head.

"I don't think it's gonna fit," she said.

"It'll fit," said DJ.

"I'm not talking about the door. Even if you make it through the door, I don't think it'll fit inside," she said.

"Don't tell me," DJ growled; "tell the boss." He nodded in the direction of Bobby, who paced around the tree, looking very worried. "He's the one drove us crazy out there measuring. He musta measured it ten times."

Ignoring Sarah's warning, DJ and Rodney began to push and shove, trying to coax the tree top-first through the door. They managed to get it no more than halfway through before it came to a sudden stop, lodged solidly in the doorway. No matter which direction or how hard they tugged, the wrinkle pine simply refused to budge. The perfect tree was now perfectly stuck.

"This ain't gonna fly, Orville," DJ panted. "Can't get it *into* the house, and now we can't even get it back *out*. Whatta you say we just decorate it here?"

Rodney took a step back and eyed the tree. "If we're gonna unstick it, we need to pull together. In unison."

DJ shrugged. "Whatever'll make you happy," he said.

Again they shouldered the tree. "Okay," said Rodney. "On my count. One, two. One, two." This time they pulled and tugged in unison—but the wrinkle pine remained firmly wedged in the doorway.

"I've got an idea," DJ said, gasping for air. "Let's count one-two-three and then pull."

"What's so special about counting to three?" Rodney asked.

"It'll surprise it. Trees can't count that high."

Rodney nodded as if he understood, but he was really just too tired to disagree.

Once again they shouldered the tree.

"You ready?" DJ asked.

"Yep."

"All right. One. Two. Three. *Pull!*"

With every fiber of their strength they pulled, and just when it seemed the wrinkle pine would never budge, DJ felt it begin to shift a little. As they gave it one last heave, it was as if the regal pine suddenly changed its mind and let go, popping back out of the doorway with such ease that it sent both boys skidding backward till they landed, regal pine and all, on the front porch.

"You see?" DJ beamed. "Don't take much to fool a tree. But now whatta we do?"

Rodney thought for a second as he tried to catch his breath. "I got an idea," he said. "What if we did it like a battering ram? Backed up and gave it a running start. Like the knights of the Round Table."

Shouldering the tree like an enormous lance, the two crusaders charged the castle. The wrinkle pine hit the front doorway at ramming speed. The supple branches near the top of the tree made a swishing sound as they sped past the door jamb, and the larger branches near the middle of the tree made a thumping sound as they bounced past; and then, just when it seemed the charge would lose its momentum, the last of the big branches, bending and straining, crashed through the doorway, and the tree burst into the house. It picked up speed as it entered the hallway and careened wildly toward the living room, knocking three generations of family photographs off a shelf, tearing off two pegs for hanging up coats, dislodging one hand-painted plaster cast of praying hands, before finally arriving at the proper corner with a shuddering stop. Silently the four children gathered to survey the damage. It was a moment before anyone spoke.

"Well," DJ said, "that went pretty smooth."

Sarah turned to Bobby. "Bobber?" she asked. "I thought you measured it."

"I did," he said. "I measured it about a hundred times."

"How did you measure it? From where to where?"

"From top to bottom," he said, his confidence now in full retreat.

"You measured from the top to the bottom of the tree? Or the bottom branch?" she asked.

"I don't remember. I think the bottom of the branches," he said.

"The tree doesn't sit on its bottom branches. Didn't

you think about that?" she asked again.

"The bottom branches!" DJ exclaimed, burying his face in his hands as if the revelation carried some terrible and far-reaching consequences. "How's anyone supposed to leave any presents under the tree if the fool thing is sitting on its bottom branches?"

"But can't you just cut the bottom?" Bobby asked.

DJ tilted his head to match the tilt of the tree as it rested against the wall. Scowling, he shook his head. "Nope. Once a tree is cut, it's cut. The only thing we can do is to cut a hole in the ceiling."

"The ceiling?" Bobby asked with a growing sense of dread.

DJ pointed to a spot on the ceiling directly above the tree. "Right up there," he said. "A three-footer. It's the only way."

Bobby looked quickly from DJ to Rodney, who simply shrugged and shook his head as if there was nothing anyone could do to help. "But . . . but it's only a little too big," he said.

"Don't matter," said DJ. "What matters is since you're

the one measured wrong, you're the one's gotta tell Dad about the ceiling."

"I reckon I'll go get the saw," Rodney said.

Sarah had been biting her tongue, but finally she could take no more and, sweeping down, she gathered Bobby up in a bear hug. "Will you stop it?" she said, looking first at DJ and then at Rodney. "You've got him worried half to death." She hugged him close and smoothed his hair. "Nobody's cutting any holes in the ceiling."

"Then I guess we better trim the bottom," DJ said, sounding crestfallen.

"We'll still need a saw," Rodney said, flashing a conspiratorial grin at DJ before heading out the back door.

When he reached the barn, he stopped. There were voices, but that wasn't what made him freeze in his tracks—it was the tone of the voices and the emotion they expressed. Drawing quietly against the wall, out of sight, Rodney listened.

"It ain't enough to say it!" It was Wylie, his voice strained with anger. "You can *say* it all night, but I don't think you got the foggiest notion how bad off we are.

Otherwise, you wouldn't even be talkin' like this."

"All I'm sayin' is we've still got some credit," Daniel answered. "That's all I'm sayin'."

"Credit?" Wylie exploded. "What credit? We're mortgaged to the rafters, best I can tell. And you're fixin' to run out and buy bicycles and fishin' poles? On credit? You lost your last nickel's worth of sense?"

"It's the first Christmas since the boy's grandma died," Daniel tried again to explain, his voice low and matter-of-fact. "I want this Christmas to be special for him. For all of us. I just want to show a little compassion, that's all."

Wylie erupted with fury, pounding the barn wall with his fist at the exact spot where Rodney huddled, causing him to stumble back away from the wall. "We're lucky to have a roof over our heads. All of us. But him especially. Taking him in like some long-lost relative. Buildin' him his own room. Makin' shelves for his books out of planks we needed for the barn. And now this? I don't know what gets into you sometimes. God help me, I don't."

There was a long pause, followed by Daniel's standard

refrain. "We'll get by somehow. We always have."

"You have said that every year since you took over running the place. Every year you say, 'We'll get by somehow.'"

"And haven't we?" Daniel asked.

"You listen to me," Wylie answered, his voice hard and bitter. "Just because we always get by doesn't mean we always will. And I'll be damned if this ain't likely the year we won't." He paused for breath, long enough for the fury to rise up again, even bigger than before. "When you were dead set on takin' him in, I figured, well, that's your choice, even though it means less for everybody. But when it comes to gambling the farm, just to show some colored boy a Christmas *you* can't afford—that's where I draw the line. How's it gonna feel when this farm is on the auction block? When all our neighbors show up to buy up everything we own at ten cents on the barrel? You gonna be happy then?"

There was a long silence from inside the barn. Rodney waited for Daniel's answer, but all he could hear was the north wind beginning to whip around the eaves.

◇ ✳ ◇

Much to Bobby's relief, the regal pine had been trimmed to fit without having to cut a hole in the ceiling. It stood majestically in the corner, filling the house with its wonderful pitchy smell. The rest of the living room had been transformed into a decorating factory, with bowls of freshly popped popcorn for stringing, shiny red and blue bulbs and boxes mounded high with tinsel, not to mention a whole congregation of little carved figures—wise men and shepherds, camels and donkeys, and angels with beatific faces blowing little golden trumpets.

Sarah strung popcorn into long garlands, Bobby placed them on the tree, and DJ and Rodney unpacked the ornaments, sorting them into piles as if they were grading apples for market. Wylie sat on the couch watching all the activity sullenly, defying any joy of the moment to rub off on him, but the argument with Daniel was still too fresh. Not even one of Rodney's stories seemed to help.

"I remember this one Christmas," Rodney began, "my Aunt Celie had come over to bring us presents. Now, Aunt Celie was a little strange."

"How was she strange?" asked Bobby.

"She used to dress up vegetables. Sew little clothes for 'em. She had an ear of corn all dressed up like Abraham Lincoln. Including the hat."

"That's pretty strange, I'll grant ya," agreed DJ.

"So this one year, she gives me this present, all wrapped up nice and everything, and I open it up and all that's there is this sweet potato. Just a sweet potato. I don't know if she was meanin' to make clothes for it and just forgot or what, but there it was. Buck nekked. Laying in the box."

"She gave you a sweet potato for Christmas?" Sarah asked. She looked up from her stringing and accidentally stuck her finger in the process. "Ouch!"

"That's what Miss Eunice said. 'Lawsa Jesus, that crazy Celie done wrapped you up a sweet potato, an' it ain't even dressed. That ain't no regular present fo' a boy.' She was really worked up about it. So she grabs it out of my lap and, muttering under her voice, heads off to the kitchen, fixin', I'm sure, to settle the matter by cookin' it up on the spot."

"Oh, no!" cried Sarah, trying not to laugh. "Poor little thing."

"Poor little thing?" exclaimed Rodney. "How 'bout me? It may have been just a sweet potato to her, but it was my Christmas present, and she'd gone running in there to the kitchen to cook it just to spite Aunt Celie. That's worse than Scrooge."

"So how'd it taste?" DJ said, as he began to hang the red bulbs on the tree.

"No, sir," Rodney said. "I was quick. I ran in there and grabbed it right out of her hands. I took it behind the house and found an old can that I filled with water and I hid it in the field until it sprouted. Then, just to make Miss Eunice mad, I used to carry it around with me like it was my prized possession. She be up on the porch, talking to somebody or other and I come by and say, kinda scary like, 'Wanna see sumptin?' They'd peek over the edge of the can, expecting a snake or a spider, and there would be this ol' sprouted sweet potato. And they'd look at me like I was crazy and ol' Miss Eunice would just shake her head and say, 'That boy took a perfectly good tater and 'fore I knows, he done made hisself a pet out of it.'"

"A pet?" cried Bobby. "You mean like a dog?"

"Better than any ol' dog," Rodney exclaimed. "You won't find no sweet potato scratching on the back door to be let in on the coldest night of the year." He smiled at the others, who had stopped their stringing and sorting and decorating to listen. "To this day, I think it was the best Christmas present I ever got."

Daniel had been listening from the kitchen doorway, watching as the others stopped to listen, smiling as the others laughed at Rodney's perfect imitation of Miss Eunice. Even crotchety old Wylie couldn't help but listen. It was a gift the boy had, this ability to tell stories that touched people. A rare and wonderful gift.

"Oh, we almost forgot the angel," Sarah called. "Come on, Grandpa," she said, crossing over to where Wylie sat on the couch and tugging on his arm. "We can't start Christmas until you place the angel."

Immediately Bobby joined in. "Come on, Grandpa. Hurry up!" He tugged and tugged on Wylie's other arm, but the old man was obstinate and refused to budge.

"Quit pullin' on me," he grumbled, and stiffly got to

his feet on his own power and headed off toward the kitchen. "I ain't interested. Let the boys do it this year." He was nearly to the kitchen door before he looked up, surprised to see Daniel blocking his path.

"Where you goin'?" Daniel asked quietly.

"To bed."

Daniel shook his head. "Not before you place the angel on the top of the tree. You heard 'em."

"Grandpa!" Bobby called again. "You gotta do it. It won't be Christmas until you place the angel."

"See? Won't be Christmas. Them's the rules," Daniel said quietly but firmly. "DJ," he called, never taking his eyes off Wylie, "help Grandpa with the ladder."

"Ladder's right here," DJ said. "Come on, Grandpa. I'll help you."

Wylie didn't move. For a long moment the two men stood eye to eye, steel to steel, before Wylie sighed and turned back. Sarah and Bobby took him by the hands and led him to the tree. DJ set up the stepladder and held it as the old man climbed. Reaching up on tiptoes, Sarah handed him the golden angel.

157

"If you didn't bring home the mighty sequoia, a normal-sized person might stand a chance around here," Wylie muttered. Stretching as far as he could, he managed to land the angel atop the tree as the others cheered and applauded.

"There! It's official. Now get me down before I break my neck!" He climbed stiffly down the ladder, turned and headed for the kitchen, pausing only long enough to glare at Daniel. "Well, at least we know Christmas ain't held up on *my* account this year," he growled.

The wrinkle pine had indeed become regal. Popcorn and cranberry strings wove through the thick green branches. Nestled between the bulbs were handmade ornaments, beautifully embroidered pieces of red and green cloth ringed with lace and string that Betsy had so carefully sewn during each pregnancy, adding the name of each child in time for Christmas. Sarah had tried in vain to match her mother's skill as she stitched in Bobby's name that first Christmas. It didn't matter that the letters were crooked; what mattered was that all three were there together, hanging in splendor, just as Betsy would have wanted.

Rodney volunteered to decorate the mantel, but it was Bobby's idea to combine pieces from all the different manger scenes into one elaborate mass nativity where a veritable army of figures now gathered in quiet adoration of the Christ child. Hand-carved shepherds stood side by side with ceramic ones, a plaster wise man leaned against a gingham camel, while an angel made of wrought iron and bright metallic paper looked down adoringly at a Mary and Joseph molded in terra-cotta and painted by hand.

"Hey, DJ," Bobby called excitedly when they had finished. "Look at our manger. We used everybody."

"Looks like Christmas in a flea market," DJ answered. "Nobody belongs with anybody."

"Looks like Christmas at the Burtons' house," Rodney corrected him, looking over at Bobby and smiling.

"I think it looks like Christmas in Canaan," Bobby said.

On the table by the sofa, Sarah had placed the

collection of snow globes. Some had scenes of Bethlehem; others had winter scenes with farmhouses and horses pulling sleighs filled with bundled and smiling people. One even had the Eiffel Tower, which DJ claimed was a big radio antenna outside of Houston just to make Sarah mad. It was fun to start at one end of the table and turn all the globes over quickly so that by the time there were blizzards in Paris, the last snow flurries were still falling in Bethlehem.

On the shelf where Wylie usually kept his books and almanacs, DJ had set up the brass mobile with trumpeting angels who, when warmed by the candles below, began to spin round and round like a carousel until the little strikers they carried rang the small bells on either side. When Sarah was little, she had called them her fire angels. She thought they moved on their own because they were so glad it was Christmas. She had cried when DJ told her about heat rising and how it was only centrifugal force that made the bells ring. Older brothers made it hard to believe in things like angels and snow flurries over Paris.

Throughout the whole house there were signs of Christmas—wreaths and bows, sprigs of mistletoe, Santa Claus and reindeer and elves. But amid all the festivities and decorations, there was one place that remained conspicuously bare—the space under the wrinkle pine itself.

Or so it seemed to Bobby as he sat dejectedly at the foot of the tree. He had been there a long time when Sarah noticed him and snuggled up alongside.

"You guardin' the tree?" she asked.

"Ain't nuthin' to guard," he said sadly. "Ain't nuthin' here at all."

Sarah rummaged around beneath the tree, trying to make it seem like there was much more to rummage through than there actually was. "Lookie here," she said, holding up a small soft package. "First one I came to has your name on it."

Bobby tried to smile without much success. "Socks," he said. "I already knew that. I always get socks."

Sarah put the package back under the tree, and when she turned to him, her voice was wistful. "Look, Bobber," she began. "It's been a pretty hard year, what with the harvest and all. It hasn't been much fun for anyone. We're all tryin' real hard to have the best Christmas we can. But you've gotta try really hard, too."

Bobby didn't answer.

"Okay?" Sarah pressed gently. "You'll try hard to make it the best Christmas ever? Promise? Between you and me?"

"Promise," Bobby said, with a voice so small and sad it was hardly worth bothering to promise at all.

"Between you and me?" Sarah pressed him.

"Yeah. I promise between you and me."

But it wasn't only between them. From the kitchen door Daniel had heard everything, and the disappointment of his son, combined with his daughter's brave attempts to help, cut at his heart so deeply he could barely stand it.

As he turned from the doorway, his eyes fell on the bright cover of the Sears, Roebuck catalog tucked into the shelf among the phone books and the seed catalogs.

Almost without thinking, he reached for it, and as he did, he felt a sudden wisp of hope—the kind of hope that didn't rely on money or weather or crops but simply on nothing else but hope itself.

Chapter Four

Some Christmas

obby had been right about the socks. They were scratchy and wool and would easily last the whole winter. For DJ there was a new pair of rawhide gloves to replace the ones that Bandit had stolen and most likely buried somewhere in the yard. There was a pretty brush-and-comb set for Sarah, to replace the brush DJ had borrowed to brush out the cockleburs buried in Bandit's coat.

For Daniel there was a large jar of his favorite lemon sour balls and another of licorice jelly beans. For Wylie there was a new tin of Windjammer tobacco for his pipe, which the family agreed smelled only slightly better than his usual Black Castle brand as he promptly filled the room with a smoky haze, forcing Sarah to open every window. Though DJ accused him of trying to fumigate the whole house, no one minded very much his trying it out. It was, after all, Christmas.

There were baseball caps for everyone, excluding Sarah, courtesy of Agri-Grow Farm Supplies. And there were Christmas cookies for everyone, courtesy of Sarah.

DJ noticed a bulky package hidden back up under the branches of the tree. Complaining loudly at the prickly ferocity of the wrinkle pine, he fished it out, read the tag and handed it over to Rodney, who accepted it sheepishly.

"You didn't need to get me anything," Rodney answered, embarrassed and feeling very much on the spot. "After all you've done for me already."

"Well, aren't you gonna open it?" Sarah asked. "Or do we have to guess what it is?"

Bobby took up the chant. "Open it! Open it! Open it!"

Carefully, almost reluctantly, Rodney pulled back the wrapping paper. Then he stopped.

"What is it? What is it?" Bobby chanted excitedly.

Rodney held up the present as if it were the gift of the Magi. "Brand-new jeans." He turned to where Daniel sat on the edge of the couch. "Thanks, Mr. Burton."

"Don't thank me. It's from all of us," Daniel said.

"Then thanks to all of you. I never had new jeans before in my whole life. Miss Eunice used to always get me secondhand jeans from ol' man Shoup. Couple times there was still somebody in 'em."

DJ snorted out laughing and even Wylie, in spite of himself, chuckled at the thought. Once the laughter died down, Rodney thanked them again.

"This has been the best Christmas of my life," he said simply.

"Well," said Daniel, climbing to his feet, "that's not quite all of it. There is a little more. Wait here." And with that he disappeared from the living room.

"Where's he goin'?" Bobby asked.

"Didn't you know?" DJ said, looking genuinely concerned. "He's gone to get your new baby brother."

Bobby's jaw dropped in amazement.

"DJ!" Sarah scolded, but it was too late to stop both DJ and Rodney from collapsing on the floor in giggles. They stopped and stared in amazement when they saw Daniel returning, his arms filled with brightly wrapped packages.

"Where did all those come from?" Sarah asked, breathless at the sight of so many gifts.

Daniel set the armload down.

"Well, that's a little bit of a story," he began. "You kids never knew your great-grandpa Burton—my daddy's daddy. Grandpa Burton loved Christmas. He loved it more than about anything else in the whole world. He'd spend all year trying to figure out what each of us was wishin' for Christmas, even little things we'd say in passing. And lo and behold, on Christmas Eve, there they were, wrapped and under the tree."

Daniel paused, looking down at the pile of gifts as if, for some reason, he struggled with whether he should even continue. The others watched curiously.

"The year I was seven," Daniel continued, "it had been a bad drought year. As bad as a lot of the old-timers could remember." He nodded toward Wylie. "You remember, Wylie?"

"Those were dust bowl years," Wylie said. "I'm surprised *you* remember."

"Oh, I remember, all right. The family didn't have a nickel to spare, let alone anything left for Christmas."

Daniel paused again, remembering, as the others waited quietly. "But, come Christmas morning? Here were all the gifts, wrapped and under the tree, just like always. Now, my grandma Burton, she 'bout had a fit. 'Where'd you get the money for all those presents?' But Grandpa, he just laughed and said, 'Don't you know, woman? Even if you're flat broke, you can still have *some* Christmas.'" Daniel's gaze fell on Wylie, who looked back at his son-in-law with what seemed equal parts surprise, resentment and shame.

"To Grandpa, 'some' Christmas meant all those things your heart wanted to give when nuthin' but your heart could afford to." He took a deep breath, looked into the eager faces and smiled. "So this year, I thought we should have 'some' Christmas, too."

Bending down, he picked up the nearest box, a square box with red foil paper, and handed it to DJ, nodding for him to open it. Carefully DJ slipped back the paper and opened the top.

It was empty except for one thing. Inside, wrapped in tissue paper, was a picture clipped from a catalog, a picture of a fisherman working a mountain stream. He wore black waders and a fisherman's vest, the kind that keeps you warm against the chill of early morning air. In his hand, a beautiful casting rod caught the glint of the morning sun.

"What is it? What is it?" Bobby asked, clambering to get a look.

"It's a Tru-flex bass rod," DJ said with hushed reverence. "With a Penn reel."

"It's just a picture!" Bobby exclaimed, thoroughly confused. "Why are you so happy over a picture?!"

"It's beautiful," DJ said, ignoring his brother.

"I've seen you eyeing it in the window every time we go to town."

"It's just what I wanted. Thanks, Dad."

Daniel smiled and handed a package wrapped with golden angels to Sarah. She began to open it as Bobby, still mystified, crowded in close to see. The box was empty except for a single picture, a clipping of a lovely pink sundress, worn by a willowy model with long hair that looked like it was spun from gold. The woman walked along a beach at sunset.

"Women are hard to shop for," Daniel apologized, "what with all the sizes and styles. I hope it's your color. It looked like you."

At first Sarah said nothing; she held the picture and looked at it as the tears began to roll silently down her cheeks. "It's perfect, Daddy," she cried, and threw her arms around him as Bobby, more mystified than ever, looked on.

The flat box with the blue wrapping went to Wylie, who wordlessly accepted it but seemed reluctant to open it, as if afraid he, too, might fall under the spell.

"Open it! Open it!" cried Bobby. "I want to see what you got!"

Cautiously Wylie tore at the paper and opened up the box, revealing a large clipping of a full-sized leather recliner complete with padded footrest. A dapper older man stretched out in obvious comfort as an attractive woman hovered nearby, cocktail and slippers in hand.

"What is it, Grandpa?" Sarah asked.

"A chair," Wylie replied.

"Not just a *chair*," Daniel corrected him. "It's a custom E-Z Boy recliner. Top grain imported leather. From Italy. You climb up in that throne, lean it back and you're the king of the mountain."

DJ reached over and, taking the clipping from Wylie, studied it approvingly. "Did you see this thing?" DJ asked, handing the picture to Rodney. "It's got four separate cyclo-massage motors. It's got as many motors as a Boeing seven-oh-seven."

"Let me see that," Wylie demanded, and without waiting for an answer, grabbed the clipping back from DJ to study it for himself. "Now what am I gonna do with four cyclone motors?" he wondered out loud, looking up into the faces of the others, who were watching with amused fascination. "Awww," Wylie growled, irritated at having found himself drawn into the magic of *some* Christmas, "you're all as crazy as your father."

"What about me? I want 'some' Christmas, too!" Bobby had been so fascinated by everyone else's present, he had nearly forgotten about himself.

Daniel picked up the biggest package of all and handed it to Bobby. It was mostly filled with newspapers, and Bobby ripped through the packing until he came to something on the bottom. It, too, was a picture.

"A bicycle!" he cried. "A red one."

"That's not any bicycle," DJ added. "That's a Stingray."

"I *know* it's a Stingray," Bobby said, appropriately annoyed, as if anyone should doubt his ability to identify a Stingray bicycle at a hundred yards in a blinding snowstorm.

"I've seen you tryin' to ride Sarah's big ol' girl's bike, dodgin' the rocks and the trees," Daniel said.

"Oh, so *that's* what's been happening to my bike!" Sarah grabbed him by the arm and would have given him an Indian burn except he twisted away at the last second.

"You little sneak," she said as he ran off laughing, waving the red Stingray at the others.

"I got a bicycle. I got a bicycle," he taunted from across the room.

Daniel waited for the roughhousing to end before handing the final package to Rodney. It was smaller than the others, wrapped with simple blue paper. Like the others, the box contained a picture, clipped from a magazine. It was a Smith Corona portable typewriter complete with extra ribbons.

Rodney stared at the clipping of the typewriter in his hand and then looked up into the face of Daniel, this man who had taken him in for no other reason than a heartfelt belief that it was the right thing to do. And now, in his own way, Daniel was giving Rodney permission to dream about being a writer. How could he have known so clearly what was in the boy's heart?

"Thought that'd make it easier for you to write down those stories of yours," Daniel said.

"Thanks, Mr. Burton," Rodney said. "I'll try and write some good things with it."

Daniel smiled. "I know you will," he said. "I reckon you can't miss."

As the family gathered around the dinner table and eagerly surveyed the Christmas dinner spread before them, everyone there sensed deep down that something miraculous had happened. Even Wylie. And while all had been prepared to make the best of a meager Christmas, who could have guessed that the miracle of *some* Christmas could unleash such power? That a handful of clippings could create such wonder?

Now, as they settled in at the table, they looked expectantly to Daniel who, in turn, nodded at Wylie. "You'll give thanks?" he asked.

Wylie cleared his throat and bowed his head, glancing up once to make sure the others were following his lead. Satisfied all were ready, he began. "We thank thee, Heavenly Father," his voice intoned, like an old patriarch on a solemn occasion, "for this food that's been prepared for the nourishment of our bodies . . ."

Hearing the words he had heard so often, DJ's thoughts drifted back to the first dinner at Miss Eunice's house when, out of distrust and anger, he had opened his eyes to take a peek and found Rodney staring back at him.

"And on this blessed Christmas Day, bless those alone or without loved ones, those in sickness or in grief," Wylie continued, faithfully, earnestly.

Rodney found himself with the overpowering desire to look at the faces around the table, to try and read the emotions as every member of the family added an unspoken blessing. As the prayer reached its crescendo, Rodney cracked open first one eyelid and then the other, just wide enough to catch DJ looking back at him. A quick smile passed between them.

"Help us," Wylie's voice slowed as if the blessing were a train steaming majestically into the station. "Help us to spend the strength that we derive from it in doing good, and in keeping thy commandments. Amen."

"Amen," the others echoed, almost in unison.

Late that night, long after the rest of the family, full and sleepy, had wandered off to bed, a small light burned in the utility shed. Rodney sat upright, Miss Eunice's quilt pulled tightly around his shoulders to keep off the chill. In his hands he held a spiral notebook. On the front in block letters were the words "FIRST CHRISTMAS."

He thought awhile before he began to write, saying each word out loud as he wrote it down, listening to the way it sounded. "Help us to spend the strength . . . ," he said slowly as he wrote ". . . in doing good . . . and in keeping thy commandments. . . ." He held the pencil motionless for a few moments, before adding a final thought. "I'm sure it didn't matter to God that the two boys peeked," he wrote. "They did it to remind themselves of how they met and how far they had come, and in the end it was just another way of saying grace."

Chapter Five

Shoup's

The glow that enveloped the Burton household lasted well into the new year. Its gradual fading was imperceptible to everyone except Rodney, who had taken a special interest in the whole idea of *some* Christmas and how it affected everyone differently.

He knew the last part was true when, several days after Christmas, he hauled the trash to the incinerator and noticed something amid the crumpled remains of the Christmas wrapping paper. It was Wylie's clipping of the E-Z Boy recliner. He stopped for a moment to smooth out the corners of the picture. It wasn't really surprising that Wylie hadn't kept it; he wasn't the sentimental type. But something about the way a memory could be so casually discarded started him thinking.

For weeks after that he kept an eye out, curious to see if anyone else would follow Wylie's lead. He didn't have long to wait. The clipping of Bobby's red bicycle showed up just after the New Year, worn and tattered, as if he had been carrying it around in his pocket ever since Christmas. DJ's early-morning fisherman didn't appear until almost February, the back scrawled with a list of things that needed to be picked up in town. That left Sarah's sundress, and Rodney had pretty well concluded that of all the presents it was the one that would never be discarded. To his surprise, it turned up in early March with something spilled on it, just like a real dress that had become too badly stained to wear.

As for the typewriter, Rodney kept it in an envelope, along with the picture of his mother he had found among Miss Eunice's things. He would take it out and look at it sometimes when he was writing in his notebooks and he wanted to imagine what it would be like to be a real writer with a typewriter. He could feel the cool, mechanical precision of the keys under his fingers. He could imagine what it was like to see his words, not written in cramped longhand, but typed on a page. Real words. Words with emotion and power. Words that someday others might read.

The spring morning was already warm and bright by the time the boys arrived at Miss Eunice's house, and the first thing Rodney did was throw open every door and window in the place, just as Miss Eunice had always done on the first day that felt like spring to her.

"A body ain't the only thing with a soul," she had said as she buzzed from room to room, opening every window before it was even halfway light outside. "This house has its own kind of soul, and from time to time you hafta air it out like you do your own God-given soul, to let the light of truth come in." Just the act of opening the windows brought back strong memories of Miss Eunice, and Rodney realized for the first time how much he missed his grandmother.

Outside, DJ busied himself picking up trash that had blown along the front of the house while Bandit watched lazily from a pool of sunlight on the porch. Later they would tend to the garden. Rodney had in mind putting in a few things, maybe just beans and tomatoes, because he knew how much it would have pleased Miss Eunice, but DJ doubted there'd be time to tend them. There was no shame in letting a garden go fallow for a season or two just to rest up. Miss Eunice would have understood that, too.

DJ took a step back and studied the house, trying to imagine what it would be like to have a place like that all to himself someday. First, he'd screen in the porch. What good is having a porch if the bugs are going to eat you alive every evening? And then there was the plumbing; an automatic pump at the wellhead would give you plenty of pressure. You'd need electricity, but that didn't have to be a big problem. He had helped Wylie rewire part of the barn, so he knew enough to handle the basics.

"Looks pretty good." Rodney arrived, sounding relieved that the house had weathered the winter so easily.

"Yeah," DJ agreed. "Built to last. Good for another hundred, at least."

"I'm just glad it made it through the winter," Rodney said, knowing nothing of houses or construction.

"You ever think about comin' back out here? To live?" DJ asked.

"Why would I come out here and live by myself? You trying to tell me something?" Rodney asked.

"I'm not trying to tell you anything," DJ said. "Just wondered, that's all."

"I thought maybe this was your way of sayin' the welcome mat's been worn a little thin at your place."

"I meant when you're older," DJ said.

"Oh," Rodney said, considering the notion seriously for the first time. "Hadn't thought about it. Not even sure what I'd do out here. I guess I *could* farm it."

DJ gave a disgusted little snort. "Farm it? Ha! You obvious ain't cut out to be a farmer."

"Then I guess I'll have to do something else," Rodney said. With rake in hand, he crossed to Miss Eunice's garden and began to work.

DJ watched him curiously. "Something else like what?" he called.

Rodney raked a brittle strand of vine into the pile before answering. "I don't know," he called without looking up, "maybe I could be a writer."

"A writer?" DJ asked as if he couldn't believe what he heard.

"Just forget it."

"No, tell me. What would you write?"

"I don't know. Stories."

DJ looked confused. "Stories? Stories about what?"

"About Canaan," Rodney said.

"Canaan?" DJ laughed. "Nobody's fool enough to pay you real money to read about this place."

Having finished the vines, Rodney went to work on what was left of last year's tomatoes. DJ, tired of shouting, sauntered over.

"You hear me?" DJ asked. "Who'd pay money to read about Canaan?"

"Yeah, I heard you. But you ever hear of John Steinbeck?"

"Who?"

"John Steinbeck. He was a famous writer who wrote about the Oklahoma dust bowl of the thirties, and lots of folks paid to read about that."

DJ thought about it while he nudged a shriveled tomato toward the pile with his toe. "Yeah, well, that's Oklahoma for ya," he said, a crooked smile on his face, the one he always saved for moments like this. "Trouble is, even Okies got more sense than to wanna read about Canaan, Texas."

Their work done, the boys headed down the back road toward Shoup's.

"Whatta you say we move out there ourselves?"

"Out where?" Rodney asked, although he knew very well where "there" was.

"Out to Miss Eunice's. It's your place now anyway. Just you and me."

"What'd we do for food?"

"We'd catch fish in Munson pond. Put in a garden. Get a cow, a few chickens. We'd live like outlaws. Anyone comes out there, we'd run 'em off."

"That's what I like to hear," Rodney said, "a man with lofty goals."

The boys slowed as they approached Shoup's. The dilapidated Mercantile was still the same, but next to it, a much larger building was going up. From the way the walls were framed, it was apparent the new structure would have lots of windows, so it couldn't just be a newer, bigger Mercantile. Everyone knew Shoup wouldn't waste money on windows simply so people could shop for beans and bailing wire.

As they got closer, they could see Shoup in front of the new building, perched precariously on top of a rickety painter's ladder, trying to nail up a sign high on the wall. LeRoy stood not far away, watching.

"What's ol' man Shoup buildin' now?" Rodney asked.

DJ tilted his head at an angle, looked, straightened it up and looked again. "Looks like a fire hazard to me."

Shoup finally managed to sink a nail into one corner of the sign and leaned back so the boys could read it. Big block letters spelled out: SHOUP'S GENUINE TEXAS PIT BAR-B-Q.

The ladder wobbled under its considerable load as Shoup tried to hold the sign level. "'At it?" he asked LeRoy.

"Naw," LeRoy said. "It's low."

Shoup raised the far corner a little, tried to lean back enough to see for himself and nearly fell off the ladder.

"How's that now? That 'bout right?"

"It's too high."

"Too high? You said it was too low."

LeRoy thought for a second. "It was the other side was too low."

"Then this side was too high already when I first asked you and you said 'too low'?" Shoup growled.

"I didn't know which side you was askin'," LeRoy said.

"The side I was fixin' to nail. The other side's already been nailed. The other side's already done."

Rodney leaned over to DJ. "LeRoy," he said, his voice low enough so only DJ could hear, "you ain't got the common sense the Good Lord Almighty gave a *duck*."

From the top of the ladder, Shoup glowered down at his son, shaking his head slowly as if the universe had given him LeRoy for the express purpose of testing his patience. "LeRoy," he said, "sometimes I think you ain't got the sense God gave a *duck*."

The boys staggered back, laughing so hard their knees nearly buckled, a sight that didn't particularly amuse the balancing sign hanger.

"What you boys laughing at?" he fumed.

"Nothing," Rodney said. "We were just wondering when you decided to, you know, put up a bar-be-cue joint?"

"Well, for yo' information, I've been thinkin' 'bout it awhile now, that's when," Shoup answered.

"Is that right?" Rodney tried hard to be serious but no matter what he did, the words seemed to come out laughing.

Shoup glared first at him and then at DJ. "What's wrong with that boy?" he demanded.

"Ah, he's just having one of his spells," DJ announced

calmly. "There's something about him that ain't quite right, but you get used to it after a while. Or try to, at least."

Shoup eyed the boys curiously. He strongly suspected they were making fun of him, but it was hard to pin down.

"You all right, boy?" Shoup asked Rodney, with a sudden sternness that straightened him right up.

"Yes, sir," Rodney said, finally catching his breath. "He just makes me laugh, that's all."

"Don't go laughing too hard, boy," Shoup said. "Some things ain't as funny as they seem." He pinned the boy with a look that made him squirm just a little.

"Yes, sir," Rodney said again, "I reckon that's true."

"So ain't this pretty big for a rib joint, all the way out here?" DJ asked, trying to change the subject and take a little heat off Rodney.

"Likely would be," Shoup replied, arching his eyebrows as if he'd given a lot of thought to that very thing. "That is, if that's all it was. But that ain't all it is. I built it big enough for other things. We can hold meetings out here if'n we want to."

"Revival meetings?" Rodney asked. "You gonna feed 'em ribs and get 'em saved?"

Shoup looked straight at Rodney, nodding his head slightly, his eyes narrowing as if to look into Rodney's deepest heart.

"Maybe," answered Shoup. "Maybe *your* soul's in need of a little revivin', boy."

Rodney felt the blood rising in his face. Who was Shoup to be suggesting anything to him about what his soul did or did not need in the way of revival?

"Miss Eunice always said there weren't a body alive couldn't stand some reviving, from time to time," Rodney said simply.

Shoup watched him a minute longer and then smiled to himself as if he had won a point. Turning back toward the sign, he lifted it into place and, level or not, drove home a ten-penny nail.

"I reckon I'll leave the reviving for the preachers," he said as he studied the sign before turning back to face the boys. The ladder shifted uncomfortably under his weight. "Don't know if you got the word, out where you live, but there's a meeting here Saturday next. Some folk comin' down from Detroit to talk about gettin' organized. Politically organized, this bein' an election year and all. Maybe you oughta come."

"Maybe I will," Rodney said. "Don't see no reason not to."

"Then we'll see you here," Shoup said. "Seven o'clock." His glance strayed to DJ, who had been watching the exchange with the strange feeling that he had become invisible. Suddenly, under Shoup's renewed glare, he knew he was visible again. Shoup regarded him as if he were little more than a curiosity before turning his gaze back to Rodney. "'Course, this friend of yourn's welcome to come, too."

Rodney returned his gaze, a slow smile creeping over his face.

"DJ ain't no friend. He's family."

Shoup thought for a second and then threw back his head and roared with laughter so hard the ladder started to topple. LeRoy ran to try and steady it. "He's family, is he?" Shoup gasped, allowing himself one more chuckle, the kind that seems warm and friendly at first but leaves an unmistakable chill. "Yes, yes, family's always welcome. That's exactly what this is," Shoup said. "This here's a *family* place."

Chapter Six

Buddy Hammer

Maybe he was just getting forgetful, but it seemed to Wylie that Earl Hammer was in as foul a mood as he could ever remember. Foul and drunk.

He had started drinking early, well before the usual time Wylie showed up for dominoes. And it didn't help matters much that Wylie hit a winning streak and won eleven straight games before it was even dark outside. But just being a bad sport didn't account for the dark mood that wrapped Earl like a malicious fog. At first Wylie tried to ignore it. Finally he asked him straight out.

"What's eating you so bad, anyways?"

"You haven't heard?"

"Heard about what?"

"They're comin', that's what."

"Who's comin'?" asked Wylie, suspecting full well he knew the answer. The news of Shoup's rib joint and the organizing meeting planned for the weekend had spread quickly through the Canaan grapevine. It had been discussed over bags of feed at the co-op and over eggs and hash at the diner. A body would have had to be stone deaf not to know about the voter registration people ol' man Shoup had invited to hold a meeting at his place.

Earl cast an accusing look across the table at Wylie. "If anyone knows it's that son-in-law of yours."

Wylie shrugged. Earl had him there. "Ah, it's nothing. Anyway, can't deny a man the right to hold a meeting. It's in the Constitution. Double fours." Wylie slapped down his domino with enthusiasm, hoping to divert Earl's interest back to the game and off this topic, which neither of them could do anything about. "Ain'tcha gonna play?"

Earl's eyes narrowed and stared coldly back at his friend. Clearly he wasn't interested in dominoes. "Any damn fool knows why Shoup built that place. Get all them *power agitators* drivin' in here. Teaching them coloreds to vote. And ol' man Shoup parading around like he's the big enchilada. They'll probably vote him mayor."

Wylie dismissed the idea with a wave of his hand as he studied his dominoes, acting like he was only half listening; unfortunately, he wasn't much of an actor. He heard the hatred in Earl's voice and knew precisely how deep the feelings ran. "You gonna rant and rave or you gonna play?" he asked finally. "Them folks want to have a meeting? Let 'em have their damn meeting. What difference does it make?"

Earl thought for a second before reaching for the bottle. He drained the last couple of swallows and, getting unsteadily to his feet, walked over and stood at the window, looking out for the longest time before he answered.

"What difference does it make? I'll tell you what difference it makes. My boy's in prison because he killed a colored while defending hisself. He didn't even have no weapon, jus' his bare hands. But you think my boy's got hisself a fair trial with that colored judge looking down at him? Them judges and lawyers and politicians. Same thing's fixin' to happen right here, and don't think it won't."

"Aw, you're just sore about your boy."

"You know, Wylie, I wonder if you'd find yourself talkin' like that if'n you folks hadn't took in that colored boy of yours in the first place?"

Earl crossed back to the table and stood looking down at his friend, holding the back of the chair to steady himself. He picked up a domino and scooted it across the table so hard it slapped up against the others, sending a few of them flying.

"Tens," he said.

Wylie looked up at him, startled, but Earl only smiled.

"So, you gonna play or ain'tcha?" he asked.

"Bobber, I want you and Grandpa to work in the barn," Daniel said as Sarah cleared away the breakfast dishes. "The siding's rotted. We've got some twelve bys you can use. And the door hinges are pulling away. If you can't get deeper screws to bite, you'll need to replace the jambs."

"There's probably not ten board feet of solid wood in that whole barn," Wylie muttered.

"By tonight, they'll be twenty," Daniel said. "You get on it today, it'll still be standing by Fourth of July." He turned to DJ and Rodney. "You boys can come with me into town. We can pick up our fertilizer."

"Sure," DJ said immediately, glad he didn't have to work with Grandpa and listen to him complain about his back and the crooks in Washington and how depressed feed prices were. He turned to Rodney. "We can have lunch at the Cock of the Walk."

Rodney nodded, but without much enthusiasm, which was unusual since the boys loved any excuse to eat at the diner.

"You don't seem too thrilled about it," DJ said.

Rodney took a deep breath. "I was just wondering, how soon are we likely to be back?"

"Likely not till after dark, Daniel answered. "Why?"

Rodney fiddled with his napkin. Something was on his mind, something that was making him uncomfortable. For all the times they had spent together, it was a side of the boy Daniel couldn't remember ever having seen.

"You got something you need to do?" Daniel asked.

Rodney sighed. "I was hoping I could go to Shoup's tonight."

"You tryin' to tell me my cookin's so bad you gotta go eat those greasy ol' ribs at Shoup's? Shame on you," Sarah teased, but her teasing was only camouflage. Even she knew about the business that night at Shoup's.

"What's at Shroup's?" Bobby asked. "Can I go?"

"There's a meeting," Rodney said. "Some people coming down from Detroit. To talk about voters' rights."

DJ looked up with an expression of surprise and perhaps a little hurt. "You wasn't *serious* about going to that?"

"I was hoping to," said Rodney.

"Why?" DJ asked, now clearly wounded. "You don't have any dealin's down there anymore. You live here now."

"Doesn't mean I don't want to go," Rodney said. "Those are people I grew up with. They're still my friends."

"I wanna go," Bobby begged. "Rodney, can I go?"

"You don't got the faintest idea what it's all about," DJ snapped angrily at his little brother, but that didn't deter Bobby.

"Can I, Pa? Can I? Please? I want to go to the meeting."

"You're not running around these roads after dark," Daniel answered, trying to make it sound like that was his only concern, but he, like the others, had heard all the talk percolating around Canaan.

"You ain't thinkin' about lettin' him go, are you?" Wylie asked. "I mean, the boy," he said, nodding in Rodney's direction without really looking at him.

Daniel turned to DJ, who looked down at his breakfast plate sullenly.

"Whatta you say, Junior? Think we can manage by ourselves in town?"

"I guess we'll have to see now, won't we?" DJ answered, not lifting his gaze.

"Well, I reckon we can manage," Daniel concluded. "Just be careful." He peered over his reading glasses at Rodney and gave him a serious look. "Okay?"

Rodney nodded.

Wylie, who had been trying his best to hold his tongue, finally ran out of patience. "I don't think that's fair," he said, the anger rising in his voice. "Do you? You think that's fair? Him goin' off to listen to a bunch of *stirpots* while you're off doing *his* chores?"

"Come on, Wylie. It's not about that. Everybody does his share and more around here. 'Cept maybe you the morning after dominoes with Earl." The others laughed, and Daniel immediately regretted saying it. He had merely wanted to make a point, but he could see the color rising in Wylie's face, and he knew it had been a mistake to try and make a joke, especially one that invoked the name of Earl.

"It just don't seem right to me," Wylie insisted, his jaw tightly set.

"Well," Daniel said, feeling a little anger of his own rising, "if you feel so strongly about personal sacrifice, why don't you skip your dominoes for one night and help us unload a few bags of Agri-Grow?"

"With my back? I'm not doing that boy's work for

him. It ain't right. And just because you make allowances for him, that still don't make it right. Maybe it's time to start asking yourself how much of what we have are you willing to give up, to coddle some boy who ain't even family? Ask yourself *that* for a change."

Shoup's Genuine Texas Pit Bar-B-Q was jumping. In truth it was more than jumping. It was jumping and hopping and skipping all at once, and if anybody had happened down the bend in the road and seen it, it would have been hard not to believe that Shoup's was the most exciting place to be in all of east Texas. There were folks everywhere milling around, greeting one another with laughter and loud voices. The music that poured from the open windows was a swampy kind of blues—part gospel, part Cajun—a backwater, soulful beat that took hold of a body and set it swaying to the rhythms, making it warm and happy and part of life again.

Rodney watched from the shadows, like a timid boy at the edge of a swimming hole, knowing how good the water would feel once he was in it, but still a little afraid to risk the plunge. He tried to tell himself it was silly to be nervous. He knew most of the people. And those he didn't know were related to someone else he did. Still, he hesitated.

The longer Rodney watched, the more he felt a strange emotion creeping over him. It was a feeling of being lost between two worlds and not really knowing how to find the way back to either one.

It wasn't that he missed seeing most of these people or even thought much about them. They had their lives and he had his. And it certainly wasn't that he felt like he didn't belong with the Burtons. The Burtons had become his family. Even Wylie seemed resigned to his living there. But still there was something. For all the changes he had made, he really hadn't changed at all. He recognized a part of himself in every face he saw. He heard himself in the ripples of laughter and cries of recognition between old friends, sounds that floated over the crowd as they waited to go inside. And in the music, as it throbbed and swayed, he felt the unmistakable rhythm of his own heart.

There was a mystery to it, and he would have liked to

stay in the shadows and ponder it, but at that very moment a woman standing near the door turned and looked in his direction and let out a scream of pure delight. His first instinct was to run.

"Rodney! Rodney Freeman! You sweet lamb! You sweet lost little lamb." Before he could move, she descended on him and enveloped him in her arms, holding him so tightly he could barely breathe before snapping him back at arm's length so she could get a better look at him.

"Look how skinny you is. Skinny as a stick. Don't them folks know to give you enough to eat?"

"Them folks don't cook like you, Aunt Celie," he gasped. "Nobody cooks like you!"

The woman threw back her head and let loose with a peal of laughter that turned every head within thirty yards. People descended on them, eager to see this boy who had disappeared so soon after Miss Eunice's funeral, scarcely leaving a trace.

"Rodney Freeman!" one of them cried. "How come you never come around? Not even to Sunday dinner." And others peppered him with questions about his new family and how things were up at the Jerrit place, while still others broke quickly away only to return moments later with shy young girls in tow.

"Rodney Freeman? Don't you remember my niece?" A pleasant woman with a large feather hat maneuvered a girl about Rodney's age in front of the boy. "This is Terrathea Turk, come all the way down from east St. Louis."

The girl smiled shyly at Rodney, who nodded and smiled back.

"Hi," he said.

"Rodney is a fine boy. Smart, too," the woman was saying as the others pressed in around them, smiling and nodding their approval.

Suddenly the music changed, and from the open windows of Shoup's poured the familiar strains of "Shall We Gather at the River," a signal that the meeting was about to begin. The crowd began to head toward the front door, where old man Shoup, wearing a white linen suit, greeted everyone personally as an honored guest at a special occasion. He paused to give a particular welcome to Rodney, grabbing the boy's hand and working his arm like a hand pump as he passed through the door, flanked by his Aunt Celie and the woman with the niece from St. Louis.

"Glad you could come, boy," Shoup said. "It's good to have you back where you belong. Back with your own folk."

Rodney didn't disagree.

Wylie stood silently on Earl Hammer's porch, listening. He had come over a little early for dominoes, anxious to get out of the house. He held his tongue as Daniel and DJ headed into town in the pickup and watched in silence as Rodney made his way down the long driveway about dusk, dressed in his Sunday clothes. But the injustice of it still made him fume with anger. He almost said something to Sarah about it as she and Bobby played Scrabble at the kitchen table, but she had shot him back such a fierce look that he only grumbled about misplacing his glasses and left it at that. Even if Earl was in another one of his moods, it had to be better than staying home and putting up with all that nonsense.

He was about to knock on the door but stopped when

he heard the voices. Drunken voices. One he knew as Earl's. The other he couldn't place, although it seemed vaguely, and uncomfortably, familiar.

Pressing his ear against the door, he listened for a moment, but it made him feel foolish, so he knocked and without waiting for an answer pushed open the door like he always did. Earl was seated at the table and, across from him, a younger man Wylie recognized immediately. No wonder the voice sounded familiar. It was Earl's boy, Buddy.

He had always been big for his age, but in the five years since Wylie had last seen him, he'd gotten even bigger. His arms were covered with tattoos, and there was a long, jagged scar across one cheek Wylie didn't remember.

Earl stumbled to his feet and called loudly. "Wylie! Git in here! You remember Buddy? He jus' got out this morning. Didn't even know about it till he showed up at the door."

"'Course I remember Buddy," Wylie said, trying hard to sound nonchalant. "Welcome home, there, young fella."

"Howdy, Wylie," Buddy answered. "Me and Pa's been expectin' ya."

"Hell, I was jus' about to come over to get ya myself," Earl said as he stumbled for the counter to pour himself another drink. "Buddy thought maybe you wasn't coming," he called back over his shoulder. "But I knew better'n that."

"Why wouldn't I?" Wylie asked. "We're still playing, ain't we?"

"Oh, we're gonna play all right," Earl chuckled. "Boy, howdy, are we gonna play."

Out of the corner of his eye, Wylie noticed Buddy sizing him up before letting out a low, dusty whistle. "He don't know?"

"Know what? What's he talking about?" Wylie moved to intercept Earl, who was heading for the kitchen table.

"About the meeting," Earl slurred. "*Our* meeting. Buddy here figured if them coloreds can hold a meeting down to Shoup's, why shouldn't we?"

"Why shouldn't we what?" Wylie asked. When Earl

didn't answer, Wylie felt a shiver run the length of his spine. "Whatcha fixin' to do, Earl?" he asked quietly.

Earl looked with bleary eyes into the concerned face of his friend. He was loving this game now, having old Wylie Jerrit going. Having him scared of what he might do. After all the times Wylie took that churchy little tone with him for saying what was really on his mind. This time Wylie was good and scared, and Earl knew it, and the knowledge made him feel all the more powerful.

"We ain't gonna do nuthin'." Earl laughed. "We're just gonna get their attention, and then we're gonna discourage them a little bit. And we need you to come along, don't we, Buddy?"

"That's right," Buddy said. "We need you to help us handle the 'attention getters.'"

"'Attention getters?'" The words struck Earl as the funniest thing he had heard in a long time. "You call 'em attention getters! That's rich!" Lopping an arm over Wylie's shoulder, Earl tried to steer him toward the door. "Come on, I'll explain it all on the way. We've got to stop over at Buddy's old place and pick up the attention getters."

Wylie didn't budge.

"What's the matter?" Earl asked, the laughter in his voice giving way to a deadening chill. "Well?"

Still Wylie didn't budge.

"I'd say he ain't coming," sneered Buddy.

"You comin' or ain'tcha?" asked Earl.

"No," said Wylie. "No, I ain't."

Buddy looked over at Earl, grinning as he slowly shook his head. "I told ya," he said. "I told ya not to count on him for nuthin'."

Wylie held out his hands as if to implore the others. "You can't jus' go down there and bust up that meeting. It ain't right."

Suddenly there was nothing but fury in Earl's face as he turned on his friend. "Ain't right?! And lockin' my boy up five years was?" he screamed. "You had half an ounce of pride you'd welcome a chance to even things up with them coloreds."

"I—I got no issue with the coloreds," Wylie stammered.

"The hell you don't, after what that son-in-law done

207

to your reputation by takin' in that boy."

Earl stood, shaking with rage, face-to-face with Wylie for what seemed like an age. Neither man said a word, but as Wylie watched, he could see the fury retreat back into the cauldron of anger that was Earl Hammer's soul.

"I got no issue with the coloreds," Wylie repeated, his voice almost a whisper.

Earl shook his head slowly, deliberately. "You're nuthin' but an old fool, and the worst part is, you don't even know it. Come on, Buddy. We got ourselves a meetin' to attend."

The two men staggered for the door, leaving Wylie alone in the middle of the living room. Outside he could hear the sound of truck doors slamming as the men climbed in and Earl cranked it up. He could hear the motor running, idling. At first Wylie thought Earl might be waiting to see if he would change his mind and join them. Or maybe Earl was waiting for him to come and talk some sense into him, like he always did whenever Earl was about to do something crazy.

"Wylie!" he heard Earl yell from the front of the house.

"Wylie, you coming? Wylie Jerrit, you ol' coon-dog." He could hear Buddy hoot in the background.

Wylie crossed to the door and marched out onto the porch, standing in plain view at the edge of the rickety railing. He'd show Earl he wasn't afraid.

Seeing him there, Earl put the old truck into reverse and with gears whining, backed it up until he was even with the porch, his face framed in the driver's window right about level with Wylie's. Earl looked at his friend, his bleary eyes full of rage. Then his face softened, as if he had suddenly remembered something.

"What's the matter, Wylie?" he said quietly, almost as if he didn't want Buddy to hear. "Ain'tcha going to try and stop me?"

Wylie didn't answer.

"After all the times you've tried to hold me back when I was fixin' to do some work, this time you don't say nuthin'. And you know why?" Earl reached out and patted Wylie on the arm like a father trying to coax an awkward confession from a boy. "Well, I do. I know exactly why. It's 'cause under that lily-white hide of yours, you want them coloreds taught a lesson bad or worse than I do. Ain't I right?"

Still Wylie didn't answer.

"I said, 'Ain't I right?'" Just as quickly as his face had softened, it suddenly grew rigid and hard and twisted with anger. "Then to hell with all of ya!" he bellowed. Popping the clutch, he spun the truck toward the driveway, spraying Wylie with a hail of gravel. Wylie could only watch as the truck, skidding from side to side, headed down the long driveway to the county road, with Buddy hooting and screaming something that Wylie couldn't make out.

"Damn fools," Wylie muttered. "They ain't gonna do nothing. It's just the whiskey talkin'. Come morning, he'll likely have forgotten all about it. That's my guess," Wylie repeated over and over, somewhere below his breath, like a prayer in search of an answer. "Come morning, he'll have forgotten all about it. That's my guess. They won't do nuthin' down at Shoup's. That's just the whiskey talkin'."

Despite the confrontation over breakfast, it had been an enjoyable enough afternoon in town for Daniel and DJ. Daniel talked shop with the farmers down at the Grain Co-op and picked up the shopping Sarah needed before stopping by the warehouse to load up the back of the truck with bags of Agri-Grow. Finally, their errands done, they headed into the parking lot under the big sign of a rooster whose neon legs strutted and eye winked and whose neon comb buzzed angrily and flickered in short-circuited glory, announcing to the world the simple pleasures of the Cock of the Walk Diner.

DJ slid into the comfortably worn red vinyl booth and pored over the menu, even though he knew it by heart and had already made up his mind on the drive into town.

"What'll it be, boys?" the waitress asked.

"I don't know," said Daniel. "Ask him. He's buying."

"I'll have a chili size, extra well done, with home fries done extra crispy and a cherry Coke with two lemons and no ice," DJ recited from memory.

"That sounds good enough to eat," Daniel said. "I'll take that, too, except for all the extra this and that. I want mine standard issue."

DJ smiled to himself as he watched his father tease the waitress. It had been a long time since they had spent any time together, just father and son, and he realized how good it made him feel.

"So we lookin' to have a good harvest this year?" DJ asked after the waitress had gone.

"We'll get by," Daniel said, leafing through one of the catalogs he had picked up at the co-op. "We always do."

"I read corn futures are up," DJ volunteered.

"Can't bank on futures," Daniel answered, turning a page. "That's just somebody guessing what the price'll be."

"But the spot market's firm. I checked that too. Grandpa showed me where to look in the paper."

Daniel looked up from his catalog, intrigued. "Why are you so interested in corn prices all of a sudden?"

DJ blushed. "I just figured . . . it's my farm, too. Someday anyway."

"Well, then," Daniel said, trying to control the pride he

felt rising in his voice, "if that's how you feel, maybe it's time you and me had a serious little talk about farming."

And talk they did. Long after the chili size had come and gone and even after two slices of fresh loganberry pie, they still talked. Not as father and son but, for the first time, as partners.

Daniel had just turned onto the long driveway when, out of nowhere, Earl's truck appeared, heading straight for them and going faster than anyone but a fool would drive on loose gravel. Instinctively Daniel spun the wheel, and the Ford swerved, skidding on the gravel and sliding sideways before coming to rest in a shallow ditch that ran along the property line.

"What in blazes—?" Daniel sputtered. "You okay?"

"Yeah, I'm all right," DJ said, climbing back onto the seat. "Wasn't that Earl? I thought tonight was dominoes."

Daniel put the truck into reverse and rocked it slowly until the rear wheels grabbed enough gravel to back out of the ditch.

"Maybe Wylie took him to the cleaners early," said

Daniel, turning for home.

"Pretty sore loser if that's the case. They don't play for more than a couple bucks. At least they didn't used to."

They were nearly to the house when, again without warning, Daniel slammed on the brakes, sending DJ flying a second time.

"What's it now?" he grumbled as he climbed back onto the seat.

"It's Wylie."

DJ looked up to see him standing motionless in the beam of the headlights, facing the truck.

"What's up with him, standing there like a post?" Daniel wondered.

"Grandpa, what did you do to Earl? He 'bout ran us off the road," DJ said as he piled out of the truck.

"They ain't gonna do nuthin," Wylie replied as if by rote. "By morning, they'll have forgotten all about it."

"Who's 'they'?" asked Daniel. "Who won't do nuthin'?"

"Earl. Earl and his boy."

"His boy?" DJ exclaimed. "Buddy's here? I thought they locked him up for good."

"Well, they didn't," said Wylie, "and now the two of them's goin' to Shoup's."

At the mention of Shoup's DJ felt his stomach tighten.

"Why Shoup's?" DJ asked, hoping the old man would have a different answer than the one swirling through his head.

"How should I know?" Wylie responded, his voice thinly stretched like a cable about to break. "They're fixin' to *convene* a meeting."

Daniel could only throw up his hands in a gesture of disbelief. "God Almighty, can't you see Buddy's just out to settle a score? Why didn't you stop 'em?"

Wylie crossed quickly to his son-in-law, grabbed him by the front of his shirt.

"Don't you think I tried?" he said between clenched teeth. "I told 'em they was crazy. I told 'em they'd be women and children there. 'You wanna hurt women and children?' That's what I told 'em. But Earl . . . I couldn't reason with Earl. Not with Buddy there. He just wouldn't listen."

DJ turned to his father. "Dad, we gotta do *something*!"

"Gotta do what?" Sarah asked from the porch, drawn by the voices.

Daniel shouldered Wylie aside, crossing quickly to Sarah. "Call the sheriff and tell him there might be trouble down at Shoup's. At the meeting."

Now it was DJ's turn to shoulder past his father to get to Sarah. "Earl Hammer's headed down there, and he's got his boy with him," he said.

"Oh, no. Not Buddy," Sarah gasped. "Not Buddy Hammer!"

"They're stoppin' first," Wylie volunteered from where he stood by the pickup. "That's what they said. They're stopping at Buddy's old place."

"Then we'll swing by there and see if we can't catch 'em," said Daniel. "Tell the sheriff to head straight for Shoup's."

"Who's Buddy?" a voice chirped from behind Sarah. It was Bobby.

"Not now, Bobber," Daniel said. "DJ, get the twelve gauge and hurry up with it."

DJ made a dash for the house with Bobby close at his heels.

"Who's Buddy? DJ? Who's Buddy?" Bobby repeated as he struggled to keep up with DJ's long strides.

DJ lifted the old Winchester out of the gun case and emptied a box of shells into his coat pocket.

"DJ, who's Buddy?"

DJ turned, brushing past his brother and nearly collided with Sarah as she headed for the telephone.

"Not now, Bobber," DJ called over his shoulder as he hurried outside. "This don't concern you."

Daniel was waiting by the Ford as DJ climbed in, slapping the shotgun into the rifle rack on the back window. Daniel turned to Wylie, who seemed transfixed.

"Wylie, get in."

Wylie looked at the other two and shook his head.

"No, I ain't goin'. I jus' don't see what good it'll do," he said.

"What good it'll do!" Daniel exploded. "You're the only one on the whole planet who can hope to talk any sense into him. That's what good it'll do. Now get in."

But still Wylie hesitated. "Won't do no good, I'm tellin' ya."

A scrambling noise came from the back of the truck and DJ spun around just in time to see Bobby disappear between the bags of Agri-Grow like a rabbit in a burrow.

DJ caught him by the back of the shirt, picked him up and set him roughly on the ground. "I said this don't concern you. Now go inside." DJ gave him a swat and sent him howling off toward the house, past Wylie, who stood resolute, still refusing to get into the truck.

"Wylie," Daniel said, his voice steeled into an ultimatum, "I don't care what you think. I don't care what good you think it'll do. All I care is that you get in this truck, and for the love of God, you best do it now."

Wylie's head dropped, like a prisoner who has just received the death sentence. Without saying a word, he climbed into the Ford and pulled shut the door as Daniel ground the motor to life.

From the porch, Bobby strained on tiptoe to watch

the Ford turn onto the county road and disappear down the two-lane blacktop toward town. Through the open door, he heard Sarah in the kitchen, making the call to the sheriff's office.

"No, I don't know what kind of trouble," she explained, the frustration rising in her voice. "I don't know who all is involved . . . exactly," she stammered, well aware that she was playing shadowboard with the truth, "but Earl's boy, Buddy, is involved. I know that much." There was a long silence. Apparently that got someone's attention. "Well, I didn't know he was out either. So then I guess you better hurry," she added. "A lot of people could get hurt."

Bobby had been pacing the porch, trying hard to make sense of all the events that were swirling around him like papers in a dust storm. It wasn't until he heard Sarah's call that the pieces suddenly fell together. *Trouble at Shoup's. Buddy Hammer. People could get hurt.* And then came the horrible realization like a blinding flash of lightning: *Shoup's was where Rodney was.*

His eyes darted around in the darkness, looking for something, anything. And what he saw was a bicycle. Sarah's bicycle, leaning against the far side of the porch. Quickly he ran to it and, holding onto the rail for balance, climbed on and pushed himself away, pedaling with all his strength down the driveway.

Before he had even gone twenty yards he heard Sarah calling him. He looked back and there she was, running after him, frantically trying to catch him, but he couldn't let her. Not when there might be trouble at Shoup's. Not when a lot of people could get hurt if someone didn't do something quickly.

Not when Shoup's was where Rodney was.

Chapter Seven

The Gathering

They drove as fast as the loaded old Ford could go, heading for the old trailer on the north side of Canaan where Buddy Hammer lived. Or had lived the last time anyone remembered. More than once Daniel turned to look at Wylie, but the old man stared straight ahead.

"They didn't say what they was gonna do?" Daniel asked.

Wylie didn't answer.

"Wylie?" Daniel asked again, his voice sharp and deliberate.

Wylie spun to face Daniel. "Huh?" he gasped. "What?"

"Did they say what they were gonna do once they got there? Once they got to Shoup's?"

Wylie looked out the windshield. "Earl said something about needin' to get folks' attention, that's all."

"Did Earl and Buddy know Rodney was goin' down to Shoup's tonight?" DJ asked. "You bother to tell them that?"

Wylie turned back suddenly, a flash of anger in his eyes. Anger or perhaps fear.

"I told you, there was no reasoning with him. Not with his boy standing there, egging him on."

"But you *did* tell him?" DJ pressed. "He knew we had family down there?"

"What damn business is it of Earl's where that boy goes, anyhow?" Wylie said angrily. "Ain't his boy."

"I guess that's right," DJ snapped. "Ain't his boy, so you let 'em go, jus' like that."

"DJ, that's enough," Daniel said. "Let's just find 'em."

The old road from the Jerrit farm to Shoup's followed a meandering creek bed that skirted the edge of Canaan.

Not many people had reason to drive down that way, and the road was seldom maintained. Much of it was rutted and worn into washboards, uncomfortable enough to ride when you could see the ruts and the holes, but with only a sliver of waxing moon to provide any light at all, it was all Bobby could do to keep Sarah's bicycle on the road.

Pedaling as fast as he dared, Bobby tried hard to settle on a plan. What would he do when he actually got to Shoup's? He hoped he could find Rodney and tell him what little he knew about the trouble. Rodney would certainly know what to do. But what worried him was what would happen if he couldn't find Rodney. What if all those people looked up to see this scrawny white boy riding into the middle of their meeting on a stupid girl's bicycle? They might just laugh in his face. Or worse, think he was the one coming to make trouble. They might decide to take it out on him.

There was no sign of life at Buddy Hammer's trailer. The windows were dark and everything was shut tight. It looked like there hadn't been a soul there for years.

"Think we missed 'em?" DJ asked.

"Unless they stopped somewhere else," Daniel said. "You sure they were coming here first?" he asked Wylie.

"That's what they said," the old man replied. "They had to pick up some attention getters."

"What's an attention getter?" DJ asked.

"How should I know?" Wylie growled. "They didn't tell me and I didn't ask."

"Well, I have an idea," Daniel said, "and I hope to God I'm wrong." Putting the Ford in gear, Daniel backed out of the driveway, turning so hard that three bags of Agri-Grow toppled off the truck bed, but Daniel didn't bother to stop and collect them. He roared down the road, silently praying they weren't too late.

It was breath-stealing hot and crowded in the meeting hall. With Celie pressed in on one side and the niece from east St. Louis pressed in on the other, Rodney could scarcely move his arms, but he hardly noticed. The very air around him seemed to rustle and churn with expectation, eager for whatever was about to happen.

The meeting started simply enough, with everyone listening politely as Reverend Cecil Robbins offered an invocation, asking for the blessings of God and the spirit of truth and justice to be present among those gathered together. Then ol' man Shoup took the podium, which was really just a choir stand someone had decorated with gold crepe paper, to give the official welcome. He thanked each and every person for coming to this important meeting and personally invited everyone back during regular business hours for the best bar-be-cue and ribs in all of east Texas.

The crowd listened attentively, their cardboard fans fluttering. Even those who thought Shoup a little pompous with his white suit and decorated music stand could forgive him his pride at having organized such a notable event. They listened appreciatively as he launched into a carefully rehearsed introduction of the evening's speaker, recounting her many campaigns and victories among the political power brokers in the great cities of the North, spoken as if he himself had organized and campaigned and suffered, shoulder to shoulder, with her and all the other brave brothers and sisters in the great state of Michigan. A few chuckled at that and a few more raised an eyebrow, not because it wasn't inspiring, but because everyone knew that Shoup had never been closer to the great state of Michigan than Oklahoma City.

As the speaker took the podium, welcomed by a rousing ovation from the crowd, the room became suddenly silent. All rustling ceased and even the cardboard fans seemed to pause in anticipation. Her name was Angela Knight, and from the very instant she began to speak, Rodney couldn't look away.

He had never heard anyone speak the way Angela Knight spoke. With conviction. With passion. It was as if Rodney had waited his whole life to witness someone like her, someone who could speak truth with simple beauty and unfathomable power, and now it was happening, in the sweltering rib place turned meeting hall on the outskirts of Canaan, Texas.

"We know where the power resides," Angela Knight told the people. "We know where the power has always resided. We know where the power resides to this day. True power resides with the people who know they *have* the power. And true power resides with people who know how to use it."

Yes, yes, the people murmured over the quiet rustle of the fans.

"But most places, people don't know they *have* the power. And in even fewer places are there people who know how to *use* their true power," she said, looking out, her voice low and dramatic, about to confide in them a long-held and cherished secret.

And the people sensed it. *Yes, yes,* they murmured in agreement.

"I know places where the black vote—the *eligible* vote—is fifty-eight percent. That's a majority. If we lived there, with that majority, we could vote in anybody we wanted. Anybody we pleased. We would have the power of the majority. And everyone knows the majority rules!"

Amen, the people murmured. *Amen.*

That's right, Rodney heard himself say, a little louder than the others. *That's right. The majority rules.*

Angela Knight grew serious. She leaned forward and looked intently into the crowd. She said nothing, searching the faces like a prophet judging for herself how ready the people might be to hear the message from the mountain. And the people looked back, intently, eager to hear.

"But you may ask why?" she started slowly. "Why in those places, in those places where our people have a fifty-one, a fifty-four, a fifty-eight, *a sixty-three percent majority vote*, we cannot get more than *thirty* percent of our people to turn out come election day?

"I'll tell you why. Our people are afraid to vote. They have been made unwelcome at the polls. They have been told they couldn't vote. Turned away. Threatened. Beaten. So we must take this fear and turn it into action. We must take this injustice and turn it into victory.

"The Constitution of the United States, that great document that guarantees *our* freedom and *our* liberty—that blessed Constitution—begins with the words: 'We the People.' It does not say, 'We, thirty percent of the people' or 'Some of the People,' or 'Only those folk who feel like gettin' out to vote.' It proclaims, 'We!' 'We the people!'"

"Amen!" shouted Rodney, his voice rising high above all the murmurs and assents and agreements. "We the people! We the people! *Amen!*"

Across the road, Earl and Buddy watched in silence, broken only by the uneven sound of Earl's truck, which was running rich and idling rough. They had a clear view of Shoup's and, although they couldn't hear the speaker, they could see the flutter of fans and the heads nodding in eager agreement at whatever was being said.

Earl reached behind the seat, slipped out a bottle of whiskey and took a long draw before handing it to Buddy, who wiped the mouth of the bottle on his sleeve, put it to his lips and drained it.

"You reckon it's time to call *our* little meeting to order?" Earl asked.

"Hell, yes," answered Buddy. "Past time, if you ask me."

Putting the truck into gear, Earl inched forward, creeping slowly until he had covered the distance to Shoup's. Close enough to hear the speaker as she talked about the glorious Constitution and Bill of Rights and hear the people respond with their chorus of *Amens*.

Buddy flicked the top of his old Zippo lighter and adjusted the flame high. Then, taking three large glass soda bottles filled to the top with kerosene and stuffed with rags, he lit the first one. Leaning out of the open truck door, he threw it as hard as he could, aiming at the large center window of Shoup's.

His aim was true.

Bobby slowed to a stop to catch his breath. He had been pedaling hard and he knew he was close to Shoup's, although in the darkness he wasn't quite sure how close. Still, his lungs burned and his legs ached from standing on the pedals. He might have rested even longer if he hadn't seen a flash from between the trees. One bright fountain of light. And then a second and a third.

Climbing back on the bike, he worked the pedals with every reserve of strength he could summon, weaving frantically, unsteadily toward the flashes of light. Even above the rasp of his own breathing he could hear screams and shouts, voices raised in anger and in pain. And all he could think of was Rodney.

Buddy and Earl hovered like grim birds of prey a hundred yards or so down the road, just close enough to see their work firsthand. Buddy sat leaning out the truck window, his face dimly lit by the glow of the fire.

He could see the front of the building engulfed in flames. People were streaming from the back doors while others climbed through windows, lifted down to safety by eager hands.

Shoup ran frantically back and forth, the flames reflecting on his white linen suit, rendering it a luminous burnished gold. He waved his hands and shouted orders, trying to organize the fleeing crowd into volunteers to fight the fire and save what was left of the building, but there was only confusion.

Earl watched through the rear window, his face tightening with fear as he sensed the destruction they had caused.

From outside the window, Buddy let out a holler.

"Look at 'er go!" he yelled. "Yee haw!"

Earl grabbed him by the shoulder and yanked him back inside the cab. "Let's get out of here," he growled. Dropping the truck in gear with a heavy metal *clunk,* Earl started down the road, fumbling for the headlight switch. Just as quickly, Buddy leaned across and angrily slapped the switch back in.

Earl swerved in the sudden darkness. "Whatta you do that for?"

"I know what I'm doin.' You want 'em to get a description?" Buddy asked.

"You want me to wrap it around a tree?" Earl said angrily.

"Shoulda let me drive if you can't see in the dark," snorted Buddy.

Earl fumbled again for the switch while turning hard around the bend in the road. Triumphantly he pulled it on. Out of the darkness appeared a flash of red and the face of a boy, hair wet with perspiration, eyes wide with surprise and fear. Earl stood on the brakes but it was too late. The worn tires skidded, and a second later came the crush of metal and the dull, sickening sound of something solid hitting the windshield.

When the dust cleared, Bobby Burton lay motionless on the ground.

For more than an hour the family huddled together in the small waiting room at Presbyterian Hospital in Clarksboro, the nearest town to Canaan that had an actual hospital.

"He gonna be all right?"

DJ, Sarah and Wylie looked up into the anxious face of Rodney. He stood just inside the door, his shirt streaked with soot and his trousers ripped in several places. He smelled strongly of smoke and singed cloth but otherwise seemed unhurt.

"He's alive, at least," DJ said.

"But he's gonna be all right?" Rodney asked again.

"Can't say. Dad's with him now."

"What about you?" Sarah asked. "You all right?"

Rodney nodded. "Shoup's is gone, though. They burned it clean to the ground."

"I figured," said DJ. "Kerosene burns hot. I've never been to a genuine Texas pit bar-be-cue before, but I didn't think what got barbecued was the customers."

"Well," said Rodney thoughtfully, his tired, drawn face softening into an attempt at a smile, "the first time you saw that place you said it was a fire hazard. Next time I'll believe you."

"Stop it! Both of you just stop it!" Sarah said bitterly. "I don't know why you think it's so funny!"

"It's not funny," replied DJ. "But what do you want us to do? Cry? Is that gonna make things any better?"

"No." She sighed. "I reckon nothing's gonna make it better."

Wylie, who had been staring quietly at the floor, suddenly struggled to his feet and crossed to where Rodney stood. "You know it was Earl that done it? Earl and his boy," Wylie announced.

Rodney simply nodded, too exhausted to express the anger that boiled inside him. "I figured as much."

"I tried to stop 'em! Soon as I knew what they were fixin' to do. I come running out the house and tried to talk him off it. I followed them clean out to the road. Ol' Earl, he 'bout run me over with the truck. I was lucky it wasn't me got hit." He reached out and took Rodney by the shoulder and shook him, not violently, but like a parent trying to get the attention of a daydreaming child. "I didn't know they was goin' to burn 'em out. I swear I didn't."

DJ gently pried Wylie's hands off Rodney's shoulders and tried to lead him back to his seat. "Grandpa, it's okay. Nobody's blamin' you for Buddy Hammer."

Wylie turned back, pushing DJ aside. "It was an accident what happened."

"Burning down Shoup's was an accident?" Rodney asked.

"Hitting Bobby was an accident. I swear Earl never would've done a thing to hurt that boy."

DJ again turned the old man back toward his seat in the waiting room. "Grandpa. You ain't helpin'."

"I'm just tryin' to explain," Wylie insisted.

"Explanations don't matter right now."

Mustering all his strength, Wylie clawed his way past DJ. "Goddamn it, let me explain something to the boy."

"It's okay," Rodney said. "Let him explain."

DJ relaxed his grip on the old man, and Wylie unsteadily approached Rodney. "It wasn't just Bobber," he said, his voice barely more than a whisper. "With the fire and all, it wasn't till this very moment you walked through that door that I knew you was safe, too. It coulda been the both of ya."

Rodney looked into the face of the old man and saw tears well up and, brimming, find their way down the leathered cheeks.

"Just—" Wylie stammered, "just because I was down there with him all them nights don't mean I had any part in this."

"I know that," Rodney said.

"We played dominoes, him and me. That's all we ever did." His voice choked off. He reached for words, for some way to explain, to give a voice to the depths of his grief. "Can't blame a fella for jus' playing dominoes, can ya?"

"No," Rodney answered, voice soft with absolution. "No one can blame a fella for that."

✧ ✳ ✧

It was nearly midnight before the double doors swung open and Daniel arrived in the waiting area, looking haggard. He brightened when he saw Rodney.

"Thank God you're all right," he said.

"I'm fine," replied Rodney. "How's Bobber?"

"They think he's gonna make it, but I guess we're not out of the woods. He's lost the feeling in his legs."

"He's paralyzed?" DJ asked. "Permanent?"

Daniel shook his head. "Doctor thinks some of it may come back, eventually. But he won't be walking anytime soon."

"Can we see him?" asked Sarah.

Daniel shook his head again. "They gave him something to make him sleep. Best see him in the morning." Reaching into his pocket, he fished out the keys to the Ford and tossed them to DJ. "Take Grandpa and Sarah and wait in the truck. I want to talk to Rodney."

DJ gave his father an odd look but didn't argue. Daniel waited until they were through the doors and headed across the parking lot before he turned to Rodney. "I didn't want to say it in front of 'em 'cause I know it would make 'em feel bad, but Bobby's all wound up about you. He keeps askin' where you are. I thought maybe it would help to show him you're okay. Then maybe he could sleep."

They made their way down the corridor, stopping at the door to Bobby's room. Rodney waited as Daniel poked his head into the room and motioned for Rodney to follow.

Bobby lay surrounded by equipment that looked to Rodney like a jungle gym, all pulleys and weights and straps that attached to his legs and waist. His left arm was secured tightly to his chest in a sling, and the side of his face was bandaged where he had fallen onto the gravel.

They stood for several moments at the foot of the bed before Bobby, sensing their presence, opened his eyes.

"Bobber?" his father said softly. "Look who's here."

"Hi, Bobber," Rodney said.

Bobby looked up and his face relaxed slowly into a broad smile.

"I tried to warn ya," Bobby said, his voice thick with the medication. "A lot of people coulda got hurt."

"I know," said Rodney. "They told me what you did."

Bobby smiled again. "It was a girl's bike." He coughed and swallowed hard, trying to clear the thickness in his throat. Daniel reached for a glass of water and held the straw for him to drink. "If I'd had my Stingray . . . I coulda beat 'em to Shoup's."

"Yep," said Rodney. "I bet you could've beat 'em easy."

"Easy," Bobby smiled again to himself and then, closing his eyes, he let himself drift. "I could've beat 'em easy."

Chapter Eight

Moses in Canaan

For Earl and Buddy, justice was swift. They were convicted of arson and attempted murder and both sent to the state prison in Anderson County. But in the days, weeks and even months that followed, it seemed all of Canaan found itself in an unending debate about the events that led to the fire and the accident.

There were those who insisted trouble was inevitable, given Buddy Hammer's return to Canaan, freshly paroled, with a score to settle. Others pointed to the violence that always seemed to follow in the wake of political organizers who came to town for no other purpose than to stir up people's emotions. Still others claimed if those same people were made to feel safe enough to vote, there would be no need for outsiders to stir things up in the first place.

Amid the lively discussion and predictions that floated out of every doorway and poured into every coffee cup in Canaan, there was, however, one consensus. The harvest looked to be the best in years.

By June the fields had grown lush and green. Warm drowsy mornings gave way to lines of thunderstorms that marched determinedly across the rolling hills of eastern Texas most every afternoon. The corn was already waist high, the stalks fat. The garden behind the house was overflowing with vegetables, summer squash and beans and tomato vines so loaded they had to be staked to keep from breaking. And over by the barn, the blackberries stood out from the vines, dark and sweet. But this particular morning the peace was about to be rudely shattered by the thunder of the Bandit express.

From behind the barn they appeared—Bandit, a rope looped around his collar, pulling the wheelchair while Bobby yelped and hollered like a rodeo cowboy. It was their favorite game. Bobby used his momentum to whip past Bandit until they were speeding side by side. Then, with practiced skill, he would fall back and let Bandit do the work until he had the speed to launch himself again.

DJ and Rodney looked up from the side of the old John Deere they were repairing and watched Bobby's dog-drawn chariot vanish over a ridge and reappear a moment later. DJ never tired of watching, and it made him feel good to see Bobby roughhouse with Bandit. He knew how hard the months following the accident had been.

In that time, some of the feeling had returned to Bobby's legs, but he still couldn't walk. Although the doctors were encouraging and the physical therapists worked hard, the more time that passed the more it seemed there would likely be no dramatic improvement. It was a reality each member of the family struggled with daily.

Suddenly there was a shout, and the boys looked up just in time to see Bobby headed straight for the watering trough, traveling faster than he could possibly steer and completely out of control. The wheelchair hit the galvanized metal trough with a resounding metallic *boom*, stopped dead in its tracks and sent the boy flying across the field like a stone from a slingshot. He hit the ground hard and, for a moment, lay motionless.

Rodney dropped his socket wrench and started for the pasture, but DJ reached out a hand to restrain him.

"Wait," he said. "Give him a second."

Rodney looked puzzled. "That was a pretty hard fall. Don'tcha think we oughta at least check on him?"

"No. Look."

Bobby sat up, looked around to get his bearings and doggedly began pulling himself along the ground, back toward the wheelchair, where Bandit stood waiting for him. Bobby reached the chair, dusted himself off and climbed back into the saddle. Grabbing the rope again, he gave it a tug and off they went.

A proud smile spread across DJ's face as he watched. "See? He's okay. That kid's going to be one tough ol' Canaan farm boy."

Rodney let out a low whistle. "Canaan," he mused out loud. "You ever wonder what possessed somebody to name this place Canaan?"

DJ knelt beside the tractor and began tugging on the tensioner again, trying to slip the new belt over the pulley. "Don't you know anything?" he asked. "Canaan's from the Bible. It means 'Land of Cowpies.'"

"It does not mean 'Land of Cowpies.' It means 'the promised land.'"

"What does?" DJ asked as he sprawled on Rodney's bed, his feet propped against the wall. He had long since forgotten the question and was not particularly interested in the answer, finding Rodney's copy of *The Catcher in the Rye* much more interesting at the moment.

"Canaan. It was the 'land of milk and honey,'" Rodney repeated, his own nose stuck in a thick reference book and his feet propped on the old pantry door, sitting on cinder blocks, which served as his desk.

"We got that," DJ said, without removing his face from the book. "We got cows and we got bees."

Rodney reached over and pulled the book out from in front of his friend's nose.

"Hey," DJ protested. "It's just gettin' good."

"Listen to this," Rodney said. "Canaan was where Moses was supposed to lead the Children of Israel."

"So?" DJ said, reaching for his book.

"Wouldn't it be funny if Moses had got all confused and showed up here? In this Canaan? Looking for the Children of Israel?"

He climbed on the bed and struck a pose, Moses just down from Sinai. "'Behold!'" Rodney boomed, in the deepest voice he could muster. "'Behold, I have come to gather my people, the Children of Israel!' And some ol' hayseed farmer sitting there, looking up at him all confused, says, 'Now, whose youngin's did ya say yer lookin' fer?'"

With a lunge, DJ managed to reclaim *The Catcher in the Rye*. "You better be writin' this stuff down," he said as he settled back to read.

"Why?"

"It's for your own protection. So when they haul you off to that loony bin over in Cherokee County, we'll have the proof to keep you there."

✧ ✲ ✧

Midnight had come and gone, and still the small desk lamp in the converted utility shed burned brightly.

This is Canaan, ain't it? This is a land of milk and honey?

Rodney paused, read back the line to himself, closed his eyes and thought for a minute.

Oh, it's Canaan, all right.

He smiled to himself as again he began to write in the notebook, one of many that lined the shelf above his desk.

We just got ourselves a little problem with the milk and honey part.

As autumn approached, what had only been hope was finally coming true for many of the farmers in Canaan. It would be a good harvest. Perhaps the best in years.

The Burtons worked hard in the fields, from before dawn to well after dusk, racing to get it all in before the weather turned. Daniel drove the harvester, with Rodney and DJ following, collecting the widows and strays. Even Bobby rolled along over the uneven ground, helping when he could and bringing the others iced tea when they were thirsty.

Daniel stood quietly at the Grain Co-op as Ralph Clark, the foreman, weighed the last load. Like always, a bone-numbing exhaustion descended on Daniel about the time the last load was being weighed. Whereas last year it seemed barely worth the trips into town, this year each load had been fat and heavy, the kernels glossy yellow. He had watched with satisfaction as load after load was emptied into the hoppers.

"That all of 'er?"

"That's it," Daniel replied.

The foreman jotted down the weight on the ticket and did a quick tally of the numbers. "I'd say it's better'n last year by maybe half again. Could be almost double. And the price solid for a change. You should do real well."

Daniel nodded. "It's the kind of year you hope to get ahead."

"Seems likely you should," the foreman said.

"We had a lot of medical expenses we hadn't counted on this year."

"Oh, with your boy. That's right. I was sorry to hear about that."

"So, I figure we're about where we were last year, more or less." He shrugged and shook his head.

"Well, keep your shirt on. They've started shipping *beaucoup* tons of grain to the Russians, so as far as prices, we may be in for a good run next couple of years."

DJ had been leaning against the truck, listening, but suddenly he spoke up. "Mr. Clark? If you figure prices are steady or better the next couple of years, why don't you guarantee our next year's crop at this year's price?"

Ralph Clark took off his cap and scratched his head.

"You mean buy from you on contract? Like we do with the big boys?"

"If that's what it means," replied DJ.

The foreman smiled. "No offense, son, but nice as you folks are, you ain't exactly the big boys."

"No, sir," DJ said. "Not yet."

Ralph Clark shot a look at Daniel, who seemed as surprised as the foreman.

"You put him up to this?" he asked.

Daniel shook his head. "Even if I thought of it I wouldn't have mustered the gumption to ask. But the boy's right. Prices go higher like you think, you could get our whole crop below market."

Ralph Clark turned back to DJ, looking very serious. "Well, son, that's a serious proposition. Let me chew on that awhile." Then he laughed and slapped Daniel on the back. " 'Not big boys yet.' That's prime. Sounds like that boy of yours got plans. I like that. I like that a lot."

With the harvest in and the weather turning colder, the time seemed right for the boys to spend a day at Miss Eunice's to close up the house for the winter.

There were a few things they knew needed doing. A spot in the roof had been damaged when a tree limb broke loose in a thunderstorm and punched a hole through the corrugated tin. There were storm windows to put on, and the upper hinge in the porch screen door was loose and could let go if the right gust of wind came along. Little chores, but necessary, and it felt good to spend a morning away from the family, just DJ and Rodney.

They started with other chores, saving the roof for last because DJ wanted the tin warm enough to make spreading the tar easy. By the time they got around to it, morning had turned to afternoon.

DJ worked carefully, cutting out a patch from a scrap piece of tin he had brought from home, while Rodney, leaning back against the warm roof, kept him company. The sun made Rodney drowsy, and he was content to let his mind wander.

"Hey, DJ?"

"Hmmm?"

"You think all the stuff that's happened to us happens to other people, too?" Rodney asked.

DJ worked the shears, trimming a little off the edge of the patch. "I dunno. Some have it better. Some have it worse. Either way I reckon it seems about the same." He tried the patch, frowned and trimmed a little more off one edge. "Why?"

Rodney didn't answer right away. "You know how everyone's always telling me to write down the things that happen? So I won't forget?"

"Yeah."

"Well, I have been. I've been doing a lot of it."

DJ tried the patch again, and this time it fit perfectly. He stretched for the can of roofing tar resting next to Rodney's leg. "Can you scoot that over?" Rodney gave the can a nudge with his toe so that DJ could reach it. Popping open the lid, he spread the gooey tar on the patch like he was icing a brownie with black frosting.

"Whatcha been writing?" DJ asked as he worked the patch into place.

"Stories. I've written a lot of stories. I also wrote a play."

"A play? I didn't know you were writin' a play. Let me guess," DJ said. "I'll bet it's about a family of crazy feed growers who took in some know-it-all Negro kid who needed a good home."

"Who'd believe any of that?" asked Rodney.

"No one, that's who. Not even me. So what's it about?"

"It's about Canaan."

"That sounds boring as dirt," DJ snorted. But then he thought about it for a second. "What about Canaan? I mean, in particular."

"It's kind of a Biblical play. It's called *Moses in Canaan.* I was telling ol' man Shoup about it. He said if I want, he'll let me put it on at his place."

DJ tapped the corners of the patch into place, making sure that plenty of tar oozed out around the edges. "I'd be careful about what you put on at Shoup's. Earl and Buddy ain't the only crackpots in town, you know."

"I was hoping I could get Wylie to come. Think he would?"

DJ thought seriously for a moment and shrugged. "Grandpa at Shoup's? Dunno. Maybe. Better ask him when he's not listening."

DJ stood, stretched and took a moment to enjoy the view. There was the beginning of color in the hardwoods. Something about the approach of autumn always made him a little sad, and this year he had been feeling it early.

"So this play you wrote?"

"Yeah?"

"I'm not in it, am I?" DJ asked. He said it with just enough disdain to make it clear he felt he deserved to be.

Rodney smiled again. "Oh, you're in it, all right. Boy, howdy, are you ever in it."

✧ ✳ ✧

The *new* Shoup's Genuine Texas Pit Bar-B-Q was even more impressive than the old one had been. It was bigger by a third and had a small outdoor patio in back. It also had a gift shop in front where one could buy Mason jars of Shoup's secret recipe sauce, as well as selected clearance items from the Mercantile next door that Shoup carted over to unload on his dining customers. But the biggest difference in the new place was apparent at first glance; the building was covered in slate-gray aluminum siding. Whether ol' Shoup chose the material as a way to state to the world that he intended never to be burned out again or simply found a great price on an odd lot of siding he wouldn't say, but everyone seemed to have a theory, and most favored the latter.

All day Daniel, DJ and Rodney worked to transform the interior of the restaurant into a makeshift theater. Along one wall they built a simple stage, complete with a scenic backdrop Sarah had painted of trees and rolling hills, featuring a prominent black cloud hovering ominously in the distance. Even if one had to use a little imagination, there was no doubt that it was Canaan. At

Bobby's suggestion, there was even a wrinkle pine visible on one of the hills.

The set, too, was simple. A cracker barrel. A couple of stiff-backed chairs on either side and, resting on top, a checkerboard.

The tables had been moved to the back, allowing more chairs to be set up in the hope that there might be a good turnout, but when folks started to arrive, it was soon obvious that any concerns about a poor showing were needless.

They came from Canaan and from East Canaan. From in town and beyond. A few drove in from as far away as Clarksboro. There were people standing in the back, craning their necks to see, and children poised atop the tables, standing on one leg and then the other, trying to get a glimpse of the stage. And still they came. There were regulars from around Shoup's but almost as many white faces in the crowd. People who knew the Burtons. Friends of DJ's and Rodney's from school. And in the middle of the front row, flanked by Daniel and Sarah, dressed in his church clothes, his white hair carefully combed back, sat none other than Wylie Jerrit.

When it seemed Shoup's couldn't hold another person, the lights suddenly went out and the crowd buzzed with eager anticipation. As the lights came back up, there was a collective gasp that broke immediately into cheering applause. Seated in one of the chairs was DJ, dressed in his most ragged overalls, and in the other, ol' man Shoup himself, wearing a flashy beaver hat and striped trousers held up with suspenders. The hat had been his idea.

Rodney had planned to dress him as a simple farmer, but Shoup objected, and there followed much negotiating about wardrobe. "Most folk know me as a man who knows to dress well. They expect it. Even though I'm play-actin', folk still know it's Shoup up there on that stage," he said.

Rodney knew he needed Shoup, not only for the use of the building but the endless free publicity Shoup generated every time he delivered a plate of smoky ribs to a table and told the hungry diners about the play he would soon be starring in. There was no doubt some people had come in hopes of seeing ol' man Shoup strutting around the stage for an hour playing himself.

"Shoup they can see any ol' day," Rodney told him. "But this'll be different. Anyone can play himself. But actors *give* performances. This'll be Shoup giving a true performance." Shoup had liked that, but not enough to give up the beaver hat.

· The audience waited as DJ and Shoup played checkers. They laughed when, for each move DJ ventured, Shoup countered with three moves of his own. DJ analyzed the checkerboard, his face a study in skepticism.

"Wait a minute. Ain't that cheatin'?" DJ asked.

"Nope," replied Shoup.

"You sure? One of them men you just jumped? He was one of your own."

Shoup nodded. "So what?"

"So what? How can you jump your own man?"

"He volunteered. Suicide mission. Certain death."

The audience roared with laughter. From the back of the crowded room, a commotion broke out, catching everyone's attention. People began a mad scurry to get out of the way, some lifting children onto tabletops, others pressing back against the already overflowing crowd. Someone or something was coming.

From where the Burtons were sitting, Daniel couldn't make out the source of the confusion until he heard a familiar loud barking. Those in the back of the room began to laugh and clap and cheer as the crowd parted, revealing Bobby dressed in frontiersman garb like Natty Bumppo in *The Deerslayer*, his wheelchair pulled to the front of the room by Bandit, tail wagging broadly from side to side.

Shoup and DJ, their checkers interrupted, looked up with dismay at the new arrivals.

"Who are you?" Shoup asked.

"I'm the Deerslayer," Bobby announced, sounding a little like the village crier. "I've been up in the hills tracking wild game, and I came across a strange traveler headin' this way."

DJ shrugged off the news, taking advantage of the distraction to jump Shoup's men twice while he wasn't looking. "Where's he from, this strange traveler of yours?" DJ drawled.

Bobby leaned toward his brother, cupping his hand and whispering loudly, "I'm no judge of distances, but from the looks of him, my guess is nowheres close." Bobby suddenly stiffened in his chair and pointed. "That's him now."

The crowd chuckled good-naturedly, but the chuckles turned to screams of laughter as, from stage right, a very strangely dressed figure made a regal entrance. His hair was powdered white, and a flowing white beard was stuck precariously to his chin. In one hand he carried a staff, which looked suspiciously like the stick Miss Eunice kept by the kitchen door to chase off snakes. In the other he held two tablets of stone, handsomely fashioned out of some of Shoup's leftover aluminum siding and hand lettered with as many commandments as could easily fit. On his feet he wore sandals made from old tires. And wrapped around his shoulders was a flowing blue plaid cape that could easily have been mistaken for the curtains in Sarah's bedroom.

Clearly it was Moses. Or more precisely, Rodney

playing Moses. He held his noble pose, waiting for the laughter to die down. DJ and Shoup could only gape at the strange apparition that towered above them.

"Holy smokes . . . ," DJ uttered.

Moses turned to face him, as if disheartened by the news. "Oh, no! Not here, too?" he said. "Everywhere I go I keep runnin' into these holy smokes. Can't go by a bush without it catchin' fire. It's gettin' embarrassin'."

"Well, who are you, stranger?" DJ asked.

"Who am I?" Rodney thundered. "I am Moses. I have come from the mountain. See?" He pointed in the direction of the black cloud painted on the backdrop. "The holy presence of God. Pillar of cloud by day. Pillar of fire by night."

Both DJ and Shoup turned to look in the direction Moses was pointing and, seeing the cloud, Shoup dismissed it with a sweeping wave of his hand. "That thing?" he said, as if this stranger had made him turn around and wrench his neck for nothing. "That cloud's just ol' Bobo up there making sour mash with that still of his. Now if you're hankering to catch a glimpse of the hereafter, I guarantee Bobo's got the stuff you're here after."

The line brought down the house. In the front row Wylie laughed so hard he could barely breathe, a loud, full, round laugh that made him shake all over. The kind of laugh that gets trapped in a man, sometimes for years, and builds and builds until, when it finally gets going, nothing can stop it.

Sweating under his costume, Rodney waited for the room to settle. The line was clever enough and he would have settled for polite chuckles rippling through the crowd. Instead, the place shook to its foundation. It was strange, he thought. Maybe these people had come because they were hungry for the comfort only laughter could give, and now they were beginning to get their fill.

"I said, why have you come?" Bobby asked. The impatience in his voice snapped Rodney back into being Moses. He tugged thoughtfully, and carefully, on his beard.

"I come to seek the encampment of my people."

"Who?" Shoup asked. "If you got people here lookin' like you, I sure ain't seen 'em. And believe me, I'd notice!"

"Not people like me. My people. The chosen people. I have been sent to lead them to the promised land. To Canaan, a land overflowing with milk and honey. This is Canaan, ain't it?"

DJ shook his head, mightily perplexed. "Well, sir," he announced, "it's Canaan all right. We just got ourselves a little problem with the milk and honey part."

"A problem?" Moses, too, looked perplexed.

"On account of the drought," Shoup added. "We had ourselves some milk and honey once. But 'fore they left, the cows got so hungry they ate up all the flowers. And the bees? Well, you can't blame the bees. If you had to buzz around all day with nuthin' to pollinate, why you'd up and leave, too!"

The crowd loved it. They cheered so hard even Shoup had to try extra hard to stay in character, fighting the little corners of his mouth that wanted to twitch up and join everyone else in laughter.

As he looked out over the sea of faces packed so tightly into his rib joint, a face caught Shoup's eye. It was the face of a young woman, dressed in city clothes, her eyes wet with laughter. Something about her seemed so familiar. She must have come the first night, the night of the fire.

"I don't think you understand," Moses continued. "I've been sent by the Lord God Almighty to find a special people, a good and decent people, and to lead them to the promised land. To Canaan. But I've been wandering for days and haven't seen a soul. What am I supposed to tell God? He doesn't kindly take no for an answer."

Shoup paused for a moment, allowing the crowd to settle in, to know that something was coming that they should hear. He stood and crossed to Moses. He reached out and clamped an arm around his shoulder and turned him to face the roomful of people—friends, neighbors, the ordinary people you see on the street, buying groceries, pumping gas, more alike than different, more good than bad. They waited eagerly, ready to hear.

"You tell the Good Lord Almighty . . . ," Shoup started, emotion catching in his voice. "You tell Him that you found the people you're lookin' for. They're already here, in Canaan. And you tell Him, too, we make our share of mistakes. And we don't always see things right. And at times we can be hateful and downright mean, like most other folk. But at the heart of it, we're good and decent. We got the promised land right here," Shoup said, his voice lowering just enough. "If only we'd see it that way. . . ."

Chapter Nine

Charlane

For nearly an hour the young woman had waited in her new Chevrolet at the turnoff to the Jerrit farm, wondering how best to attempt what she intended to do. Now, as she stood on the front porch and faced the weathered door, she wondered again. Although she had watched Rodney in the play the night before, it would be the first time he would see her in more than sixteen years.

That very morning in her motel room off the Interstate, she had stood a long time looking at herself in the mirror. She had tried to imagine herself as he might see her, tried to soften the lines trouble had etched in her still-young face. She had always been pretty, a girl with proud features, as Miss Eunice's features had been proud. But now there was a sadness in her face, mostly around her eyes, that made her beauty seem more fragile.

Gathering her courage, the young woman pulled open the screen door and knocked firmly. After what seemed like an age, the door opened and Sarah stood in the doorway.

"Yes?" Sarah asked. She couldn't hide her surprise that a black woman dressed in nice city clothes would have found her way to the Burton door.

"I'm Charlane Washington," the woman said.

Sarah nodded as if there surely must be more, but the woman simply waited.

"Yes?" Sarah asked again.

"Charlane *Freeman* Washington," she said.

Daniel, who had been in the kitchen, joined Sarah in the doorway.

"Charlane Freeman? You're Eunice Freeman's daughter?" he asked.

"Yes," the woman said. "I'm Rodney's mother."

Daniel stood speechless, staring into the face of the woman. He had always suspected one day she might return for Rodney and had tried to prepare himself for that moment if it ever happened.

"Please come in," he heard himself say.

They settled in the living room, Daniel and Charlane, as Sarah dutifully brought in tall glasses of lemonade and freshly baked oatmeal cookies before retreating to the kitchen, where she busied herself with fixing dinner, all the while straining to hear the conversation from the next room.

"I was seventeen when I had Rodney," Charlane began. "I was not married at that time, and Miss Eunice was able to provide for him a home such as I couldn't do."

Daniel nodded. "We all knew she had a daughter somewhere. But when Miss Eunice passed away, no one knew how to get in touch. I guess you hadn't stayed close."

Charlane had to laugh. "Close? The farther the better in those days. Miss Eunice said I was like a wild thing even the devil himself couldn't tame." She put her hands up like a fugitive might to indicate surrender.

Daniel smiled and shook his head. "It's not an unpardonable sin, growin' up a little wild. I'm sure we all sowed our share of wild oats. I'm sure you and Miss Eunice could have worked it out, once you had grown up some."

"Mr. Burton," she said, looking up into the weathered, handsome face of the farmer, a man whose kindness she could only imagine and upon whose doorstep she had arrived unannounced, intent on changing everything. "I didn't come here to talk about me and Miss Eunice. I came here to see my boy."

Daniel stood and indicated for the woman to follow as he led her through the kitchen to the back porch. There they arrived just as Rodney and DJ happened around the corner of the barn and turned toward the house, their evening chores finished. Unaware, the boys stopped midway between the house and barn. They joked and shoved, and suddenly Rodney grabbed DJ by the waist and tried to wrestle him to the ground. DJ quickly countered by grabbing Rodney's shoulders, but DJ was far too heavy and Rodney far too tall, and the result was more like a dance,

Rodney tugging and pulling, DJ pushing and resisting, laughing and taunting as Bandit circled the two, barking. Finally, more from dizziness than exhaustion, the two friends tumbled into a heap, too weak from laughter even to move.

Daniel glanced once or twice at Charlene, this woman who watched so intently. The reunion she must have dreamed about so often was now within her grasp, her boy almost close enough to touch. But still she seemed afraid.

"You want I should call him over?" Daniel asked.

Gratefully she nodded.

"Rodney!" he called. "Someone to see you!"

Both boys looked up and scrambled to their feet, jogging easily toward the house. They were close to the back porch before either one of them could make out the visitor.

As Rodney got within a hundred paces, he slowed; the sight of a pretty black woman in city clothes standing beside Daniel Burton was unexpected. As he got closer still, he felt an odd sensation. His mouth seemed to go dry and he felt his pulse quicken. Even before she spoke, he knew.

"Hello, Rodney," the woman said.

Rodney stopped and looked carefully at this woman who reached out her hands to him, her eyes brimming with tears. He recognized her from the photograph he had taken from Miss Eunice's things. He sensed in her the very emotion Miss Eunice had captured in the image of the little girl on the quilt, the hope mixed with sadness, the pride and passion. Most of all, in her face he could clearly see his own face, the same intelligence, the same fire.

Charlane bounded from the porch and threw her arms around him, only to hold him at arm's length to look at him all over again, up close.

"Just look at you, my baby! All grown up. Looking so much like your mama. There's no mistaking you any-where."

Overcome with shyness, Rodney stared at his feet. "W-w-what are you doing here?" he stammered.

"Why, baby, didn't you get my letters?"

"I got one you sent when I was six."

"Miss Eunice said she didn't want me writing and if'n I did she'd throw them all away, so's I'm glad you got one. But if you had got the others you'd know I'm married now. To a good man. A navy man. We got ourselves a big house in California, and I've come to ask you home to live with us. Isn't that wonderful?"

But it wasn't wonderful. At least not to DJ, who had been witnessing the tearful reunion with initial confusion followed by a growing sense of alarm. "Hold on a minute," he said, approaching Daniel like an attorney approaching the judge. "She can't just come in here and take him off, whoever she thinks she is."

"I'm his mother," Charlane answered. "A boy belongs with his mother."

DJ turned from Daniel to face her; he didn't waste time trying to be polite. "That right? A boy belongs with his mother? Well, lady, no one's seen you for some sixteen years. Where were you when Miss Eunice died? Where were you when there wasn't another soul to take him in?"

"DJ . . . ," Daniel warned. "Let's not go running away with ourselves here."

"Well, I never laid eyes on her before. I don't know if she's his real mother. I don't know nuthin' about her." He stormed back from the porch railing to where the others stood. "If you think we're gonna just let some stranger waltz in here and take him off, you're outta your tree!"

"She *is* my mother," Rodney volunteered.

"You stay out of this," DJ snapped. "Who she is ain't the point right now."

"DJ," Daniel said, "it ain't up to us."

"Whatta you mean, 'it ain't up to us'?"

Daniel sighed. "We never had a claim on the boy."

"Being part of a family ain't a claim?"

"Not a legal claim," Daniel said. "She's his mother. She's his legal family."

While Daniel and DJ argued, Charlane used the time to compose herself and to remember what she had intended to say—what she had practiced. She wanted to tell them how thankful she was for all the Burtons had done. How it had been a godsend that this family had been there to take care of her boy at a time of crisis. More than anything, she wanted them to know that.

"Don't you see?" she began, her voice softer and warmer. "God gave me this child even though I couldn't do right by him before. And that's why, I believe, God put him in your care until I could. And now I can."

"This is his home. This is where he wants to stay," DJ said angrily. "Right here."

"I say let the boy decide!" a voice boomed, as if a clap of thunder had loosened directly overhead. It was Wylie. He stood calmly by the edge of the porch, his arms folded across his chest like a drugstore Indian. "Reckon he's old enough to choose what's best for him, all by himself. Old enough and, God knows, he's smart enough." Wylie ambled toward the others, stopping next to Charlane. He gave her a kindly nod and a smile. "All this is plowed pretty fresh. I say give the boy a chance to sleep on it," he said.

"I didn't come all this way . . . ," she started to protest, but Wylie cut her off with a little wave of his hand.

"It don't matter how far you came. What matters is

what's best for the boy," he said, giving her another kindly smile, but his voice left little room for further negotiations. "I say give him till the morning. That's plenty soon enough to decide."

Sarah rarely showed her anger. Not that she didn't feel it every bit as strongly as all the other emotions she shared so generously with everyone around her—her joys, and the swelling sense of pride she felt when someone she loved did something brave or unselfish. She even sometimes shared her sadness and frustration at all those things in life that seemed cruel and unnecessary. But almost never her anger. It just wasn't her way.

All through Charlane Washington's visit, Sarah remained quietly in the background, listening intently when she wasn't busy fixing dinner or making a new pitcher of lemonade or patching the knee of Bobby's jeans. Even when Charlane graciously declined Daniel's invitation to stay for supper and, after kissing Rodney's cheek, disappeared back down the long driveway, Sarah watched in silence, daring not to fashion her feelings into words.

But amid the unnatural quietness that descended on the Burtons' dinner table, it was unlikely anyone even noticed.

Rodney had asked to be excused even before dessert and hadn't been seen since. DJ and Bobby headed for bed early, and Wylie had turned in well before nine, claiming his back was bothering him. That left only Daniel and Sarah.

Leaning on the rail of the back porch, Daniel let his eyes wander out over the fields, bare and bright in the light of the waning harvest moon. It was where he usually went when there was thinking to do. Many times he had kept a vigil long into the night when there was something troubling him. Tonight promised to be one of those nights.

He heard the kitchen door close softly, but he scarcely turned as Sarah stepped onto the porch. They stood together for what seemed a long time, the comfort of sharing the silence far outweighing any need to break it. Overhead an eastbound jet, growling softly, marked the sky with an icy trail made silver by moon. Somewhere near the creek a great horned owl called to its mate with a series of *hoot*s, each one louder and more insistent than the one before.

"You gonna let her just come in here and take him off?" Sarah turned away from the night to face her father. "What do you know about her? What do any of us know? Not a single thing."

"Only what she told us," Daniel answered. "That she loves her boy. Misses him. Wants to make things right."

"But what kind of mother would she be?"

Daniel thought for a second, frowned. "Nobody can answer that but her. On the other hand, he is nearly grown. I doubt she could change him much these days even if she tried. Miss Eunice did too good a job with him early."

"Like we've done ever since," Sarah reminded him.

"Maybe," Daniel replied. "I like to think maybe we made a difference. I don't know."

"To just waltz in here without a word of warnin' and snatch him up! Announce that she was takin' him off like we were nuthin' more than foster care!" Sarah fumed, not bothering to curb the flood of anger she had spent all afternoon damming up. "How dare she treat us like that? She has no right!"

"She is the boy's mother."

"That still don't give her the right to break up this family!" With an angry toss of her head, she stormed off toward the barn. Daniel let her go, watching as she threw open the barn door and disappeared inside.

"Her mother'd be mighty proud of that one," he mused. "She's held this family together. And she's still trying."

It didn't take Daniel long to find her, in the far corner of the barn, sitting in the same stall they had first put Bandit in so many years ago. She was crying softly, and Daniel said nothing, just put his arm around her for what seemed like a long time until finally her breathing was easier and he knew she had cried her fill.

"You think just because we love the boy that's strong enough reason to hold him here?" he asked.

She seemed surprised at the question. "What other reason is there? He's family."

Daniel smiled and shook his head. "I don't know, sister," he said. "Sometimes I think there's nothing in Canaan strong enough to hold him. Can you picture him crop farming the rest of his life? Scrawny little bean pole?"

"Miss Eunice wasn't a farmer, and she did all right out there."

"Miss Eunice was tied to that land," Daniel said. "Tied to it like we're tied to this. It's all we've got and all we're ever likely to get. So it's our job to work it the best we can." Daniel walked to the window and stood for a moment looking out, far beyond the fields and hills and even beyond Canaan. "That boy's got a whole world yet to know, bright as he is. A world beyond what you and me can even imagine. He sees it. I know he sees it. And it's his job to work *those* fields the best he can, jus' like we do *ours*."

Daniel paused to take one last look into the autumn night before turning back to Sarah. "Maybe this is God's way of tellin' him it's best he get a start on it."

Chapter Ten

The Disappearance

"He's gone."

The words jolted into Daniel's consciousness at exactly the same moment Bobby's wheelchair collided with the frame of Daniel's bed.

"His things?" Daniel asked as soon as he could gather his wits and scramble out of bed. Tucking his nightshirt in a pair of jeans, he headed for the back porch. "Just him? Or did he take his things?"

"He didn't take nothing," Bobby said. "It's all still there."

Rounding the house, Daniel nearly collided with DJ.

"Rodney's gone," Daniel said.

"I know." DJ seemed surprisingly calm at the news.

"You knew he was going?"

"Nope," said DJ. "But I ain't shocked he did. I figured he might."

Daniel looked perplexed. "And jus' whatta we supposed to tell his mama, who's due to show up in an hour, expecting an answer?"

"I'll find him," DJ said.

"You know where he is?"

"I got a pretty good idea."

Miss Eunice's house looked so still in the early morning light, it was almost as if it had been painted against the fading autumn colors of the hardwood trees. DJ stood quietly watching the house, waiting to see if anything stirred. With deliberate slowness he covered the distance to the wooden porch and tried the door. It was locked.

Had he been wrong about finding Rodney here? He knew his friend. His mind and his heart. There could be no other place he would have gone. As he turned the corner of the house, he stopped and a smile crept over his face. No, he hadn't been wrong.

Rodney looked up from the top step of the small kitchen porch as DJ arrived, almost like he had been expecting him.

"Well, boy, you coming or not?"

Rodney raised his eyebrows. "I look like your boy?"

"Tell ya the truth, I'm too tired to guess." DJ settled onto the middle step and slowly shook his head as he looked out over Miss Eunice's garden, now fallow. "You know all the times I've been sayin' we should move out here? Maybe we really *should* move out here. That'd solve the whole thing."

"It would?" Rodney asked.

"Sure. Tell the whole world this is your real house. This is where you belong. What could she say?"

Rodney thought for a second. The sun was just hitting the top of the elm tree, now largely bare. "All morning I've been thinking," he said. "In sixteen years, I've never been farther west than Wichita Falls. And that's when I was nine."

"So? What's west of Wichita Falls that's such a big deal?"

"Oakland, for one. That's where my mother lives. Oakland, California. You know where that's near? That's near where John Steinbeck lived. And Jack London. That's near where Stanford University is. And Berkeley. University of California at Berkeley. Can you think what it would be like to live near all those places?"

"There are colleges in Texas, you know," DJ countered. "Good ones. Even in east Texas. I betcha they all teach the same stuff. Or not enough difference to matter."

Rodney nodded. He *had* thought about that. He had thought about all of it. And the more he thought, the more he came to the same conclusion. Whatever he decided, there would be something lost, someone left behind. There was no escaping it.

"The way I figure it," Rodney began, speaking slowly, thoughtfully, as if to say to DJ that this was what he had decided and it likely wouldn't change, "I lived a couple years with you. I oughta live a couple of years with her."

"Why?" DJ asked. "Why do that?"

Rodney smiled. "Equal punishment. Just like in fifth grade."

"Guess if I'd done my homework that day, none of this would be happenin'. That what you're trying to tell me?"

"If you'd have shut up and written down Albany like I told you, none of this would be happenin'. That's what started it, if you'd bother to remember."

DJ shook his head, totally unwilling to concede the point. "Well, how was I supposed to know you knew Albany from a pucky pile?" he asked.

The corners of Rodney's mouth edged into a smile. "You remember Miss Eunice? The lady that used to live here?"

"Yeah. I remember Miss Eunice."

"Well," Rodney said, the smile now broadening into a grin, "Miss Eunice, you see, she was *born* in Albany."

The autumn-brown Chevrolet Impala had been carefully packed with as many of Rodney's things as would fit. There wasn't that much he needed to take, especially since he'd be coming back to Canaan eventually—just his clothes and a few things his grandmother had given him. And, of course, there were the books. He couldn't take them all. They would have easily filled the car and left room for nothing else. In the end, after much thought, he settled on just enough to fill four cardboard boxes and left the rest for the Burtons to use until he returned.

It was late morning before the car was packed. The Burtons helped with the packing and generally tried to be cheerful, but it was hard duty. Finally, as the last items were snugged into place, they gathered, standing as if posed along the porch: Daniel looking thoughtful, resting his hand on Sarah's shoulder; Wylie standing like a soldier at parade rest, his hands clasped behind him; Bobby rolling nervously in his chair, playing fetch with Bandit, who barked and pawed the ground, sensing something momentous about to happen.

DJ waited by the car. "Think you'll be out of here before noon?" He handed the last remaining box to Rodney, who stuffed it into the backseat.

"You want me gone that quick?" Rodney asked.

"I jus' figure if you're gonna stay away for two years and

you leave before noon, today counts as a day. So that'd be one less." DJ shrugged. "A lot can happen in a day."

"Then I guess we better go." Rodney slammed the door as if to settle the point.

Charlane crossed to Daniel and held out her hand graciously, and Daniel held it firmly for a moment or two. He looked beyond her to where Rodney waited by the car with DJ. Seeing him look, she turned to look, too.

"He's nearly a man," she said, more to herself than anyone. "Very nearly a man. Makes me proud just seeing him." She turned back to Daniel, and there were tears in her eyes. "I'm grateful you did such a good job keeping him. Very grateful."

"I know he'll be a blessing to you, ma'am," Daniel said. "God knows he's been that to us. A blessing and more."

She called to the boy. "Rodney, it's late. Come say your good-byes to these folk."

Rodney approached Daniel and held out his hand, but Daniel didn't bother with that. He folded the boy into his arms and held him in a bear hug for what seemed like an age.

"You keep writin'," he told him. "Y'hear?"

Rodney nodded. "Yes, sir. I will. And I'll be back come a year next October."

"Come back here and we'll put ya to work," Daniel said as he slapped him gently on the back. "Make you earn your keep."

Sarah held him close and cried softly into his shoulder. "Send us letters," she said. "And pictures. I'd like a picture of the Golden Gate Bridge."

"I'll write every week," he said.

He turned to Bobby and Bandit, who had grown tired of fetch, and sat panting in the sunshine.

"Bye, Bobber," he said.

"Bye," he answered, trying hard to be brave and not cry like his sister had. "Write some more stories about us, okay?"

"Okay," Rodney said. "And you need to keep working those legs. They'll get stronger and stronger if you keep at it. Okay?"

"Okay," Bobby answered.

Wylie watched the scene with detached curiosity, as if

he were watching himself in a dream, but before Rodney could get to him, Wylie turned away, fumbling for the screen door and disappearing into the quiet safety of the house.

"He didn't mean anything by that," Daniel said, first to Charlane, then to Rodney. "He's not been feelin' well lately. And today, with the excitement and all . . . I know he'll miss ya."

Rodney nodded. Whatever his mistakes and shortcomings, Wylie had paid for them with his soul in ways the rest of them might never understand. "Tell him goodbye," he said. "I'll see him a year come October."

Rodney crossed back to where DJ stood waiting by the car.

"So, you reckon this is it?" DJ asked.

"You'll look after the old place while I'm gone?"

DJ thought for second. "I've been meanin' to talk to you about that. I've been thinking once you're gone about maybe turnin' it into a Cajun joint. Give Shoup a run for his money."

Rodney smiled. "Thought you and me were gonna live there. How can we live there if you've turned it into a Cajun joint?"

DJ shrugged and sighed, as if life had just thrown him yet another complication. "Well, if you feel that strongly about it, I reckon we just better leave it as is."

Over by the corner of the house, Bandit had begun barking at a fat red squirrel who happened down a tree. Rodney called to him, and he came running to the boys. Rodney reached down and patted his warm, shiny coat and scratched his belly. "Take care of Bandit," Rodney reminded DJ. "He's my dog, too, remember?"

"I remember," DJ said. "If it wasn't for me, you'd have named the poor guy Lazarus."

Charlane approached the car, keys in hand. The look on her face left no doubt she was eager to go. "Rodney?" she urged softly. "We have a long drive. Best finish your good-byes."

Rodney shrugged and looked down at his shoes, making a circle in the gravel with first one toe and then the other. "Well, I guess I'll see ya," he said.

"Yeah, see ya," DJ answered. "Or as we say in Texas, *adios, amigos*."

"*Adios*," Rodney answered. "Or as *we* say in Texas, don't eat any skunk."

Charlane slipped the key into the ignition and started up the car.

"Rodney?" she urged, a slightest hint of urgency rising in her voice. Maybe it *was* the long drive that made her so anxious, or maybe it was that nagging feeling that reminded her of all the times before when she had wanted so desperately to take him to live with her but hadn't. Until they were safely away from Canaan, Rodney would never be completely hers. Rodney was barely in the car before she put the Impala into drive and began to inch down the long gravel driveway.

But before the car gained speed, there came a noise from the house, a shout loud enough for everyone to hear. Even Rodney. He turned and poked his head out the window. Wylie was running toward the car. His hands were cupped around his mouth and he was yelling something.

It sounded like a phrase. Repeated over and over.

"Don't forget . . . ," he seemed to be saying. "Don't forget . . ." Rodney couldn't make out the rest of it.

"What?" Rodney yelled back as he hung out the passenger window.

"Don't forget . . . !" Wylie continued running toward the car, the rest drowned out by the sound of tires on the gravel road.

Rodney ducked back inside the car. "Stop the car!" Rodney shouted at Charlane, his voice so full of authority that she stood on the brake. The car skidded to a stop.

It took several moments for Wylie to get to the Impala. He stood, breathing heavily and holding one hand to his chest. "A place . . . ," he said, gasping. "Don't forget . . . you've always got a place. Here . . . No matter where you go . . . don't forget . . . you've family . . . You've always got a home . . ."

Book Three

The Promise

Chapter One

Opening Night

W e're lucky to have a roof over our heads," a voice boomed, gruff and menacing. "Him especially. Taking him in like he's a long-lost relative."

A thin black boy with a serious look stood by the side of the barn. He seemed at first afraid, looking for somewhere to hide, but then grew curious and huddled closer to the wall, hoping to hear what the voices inside were saying.

"We'll get by somehow," another voice said reassuringly. "We always have."

From out of nowhere, a third man appeared. He had

long scraggly hair that stuck out in all directions from under a black beret, and he carried a notebook stuffed fat with so many pages it looked like a book. He talked in a fast, loud voice, as if addressing a whole roomful of people.

"We need to play this scene less angry and more ironic," he said with a sweeping gesture of his hand. "Wylie? I need you to feel your anger, but don't release it so much. Not so early."

Two heads popped around the wall of the barn, which was only a stage barn.

"How angry do you want?" asked a man who looked nothing like Wylie. "The family's broke. He's blaming Daniel. Seems like he should be plenty angry."

The man with the notebook pressed his fingers to his face as if he were thinking hard. "Angry, yes," he said. "But deeper. More frustration. Like a molten volcano. You could blow at any minute. But maybe not. You see my point?"

The Wylie who didn't look like Wylie seemed confused. "All I know is angry or not angry. I don't know volcanoes. Maybe you need a geologist to play this part."

From his perch in the darkened balcony of the old

theater, Rodney Freeman smiled. Sitting through a rehearsal for one of his plays never failed to teach him something about himself. Even though the people onstage were not the real people, the emotions they generated were often so unerringly real, and the truth they conveyed so powerful, that when he closed his eyes, it was as though he were back outside that barn, huddled against that rough-sided wall, listening to Wylie and Daniel argue.

Eight years. It felt like a short lifetime. Rodney had grown taller and filled out some. His boyish features had sharpened into the face of a man, handsome and intelligent. His clothes were stylish and carefully chosen. To see him, one would think he had always lived in the city, and to those who knew him or heard him interviewed or came to see his plays, it was hard to believe that this carefully spoken young playwright had grown up in a place as remote as Canaan, Texas. For Rodney, the move to California had been a watershed, a journey to a world he could not have imagined.

The adjustment hadn't been easy. Night after night he would stare out at the Oakland skyline and dream of the rolling hills of east Texas, the pure air and the stillness of the winter sky. And of course he missed the Burtons.

True to her word, Charlane had done everything in her power to make her son welcome. Often, when her husband was away at sea, they would cross the Bay Bridge to the city, to wander through museums and attend concerts. He learned to love the waterfront along Embarcadero and the view of the city from Coit Tower. On weekends they would drive into the Napa valley or south to Monterey, to explore what remained of John Steinbeck's Cannery Row and imagine life on Tortilla Flat.

As summer approached, Charlane urged Rodney to apply for a scholarship to the university. Instead, he chose to join a small theater workshop. If Charlane was disappointed by the decision, she was careful not to show it. Where better for a young writer to learn than in the ambitious company of other playwrights, actors and directors?

His first plays had been simple, written with humor and performed by student theater groups. But as his confidence grew, more ambitious works followed. He wrote a play called *Angela* about a political activist from the North who shows up in Canaan to organize the townspeople, and *Last Stop*, a play about an old black conductor on the 20th Century Limited who was forced to retire because he was getting too senile.

By the time he had finished *The East Texas Trilogy*, three plays about the plight of the American farmer, the critics were already hailing Rod Freeman as a bold new voice in American theater. With that, success had come blindingly fast.

A young woman approached his row in the empty balcony and crossed to where he was sitting.

"Mr. Freeman?" She offered her hand. "I'm Cynthia Barlow from the *Chronicle*."

Rodney took her hand warmly. "Good to see you again," he said. "Would you like to go somewhere quiet? I know just the place."

The coffee shop around the corner from the Cullen Playhouse was a good place to talk. The hostess recognized the young playwright and steered them toward a booth in the back where they wouldn't be disturbed.

"Your new play," the reporter began, "*Christmas in Canaan,* deals with growing up in the same small Texas town, but you have said it is much more personal than your earlier plays. More soul-searching. Why?" She adjusted the microphone of a small tape recorder.

Rodney took a sip of coffee and thought for a moment. "*Christmas in Canaan* is about the first Christmas after I was taken in by the Burton family. There *was* a lot of soul-searching. It was a very serious time. We didn't know if we'd lose the farm. But it was also a very wonderful time."

"As you watch people portraying you and the family you lived with, what goes through your mind?" she asked.

"What goes through my mind is how uncommon their love was, not only for me but for anyone else who needed it. Old man Shoup, whose place got burned down. Even Earl Hammer, the neighbor who lived next door and was as hateful a human being as you'd ever meet. After he was convicted for his part in the fire, every Christmas Sarah Burton would bake cookies for him and bring them to the prison. Didn't matter what he had done—he was still a neighbor. That's how the grandfather died. Had a heart attack on the way up to take Earl and Buddy some Christmas cookies."

Rodney poured a little cream into his coffee and watched as it made small white clouds before he stirred it in. "That's the one regret I have. I wish I could have told him how much what he said meant to me."

"Who?" the reported asked.

"Wylie Jerrit. The day I left, he chased down the car just to tell me that no matter what happened, I would always have a place there. With them." Rodney held his coffee cup in front of his face and felt the warmth radiate from the cup. "I've thought of that a thousand times. How important it is to have a place. A place where you're loved. Accepted. I wish I could have told him that."

The reporter reached into her satchel and brought out a manila folder. In it were clippings from various newspapers, articles about Rod Freeman and reviews of some of his plays. She shuffled through the clippings until she found the one she was looking for.

"One critic writes of you," she said, "and I quote: 'For

all the talk of his humble origins, Rod Freeman is little more than a clever opportunist, a scavenger sifting through the rubble of his childhood, looking for glittering moments.'" She looked up, saw him listening intently. "Do you ever feel you've taken advantage of those people you've left behind?"

He thought for a moment before he answered. The question had struck a nerve, and the reporter could sense it.

"There's not a day goes by that I don't think about those people," Rodney said, surprised at the edge he heard in his voice. "What they were willing to sacrifice to do what they believed was right. It's something I carry with me. I'll always carry it with me."

The reporter waited. She knew the importance of letting people experience the fallout from their own self-revelation before moving on. Invariably that's where the real story was.

"Do you ever get back to see them?" she asked finally.

"Not for a while," Rodney answered.

Sensing something, she pressed a little deeper. "How long?"

"A while," he repeated.

Again there was that tension, that guardedness. Trusting her instincts, she pressed deeper still. "How many times since you left? A dozen? A couple? Ever?"

Rodney didn't answer, and in the silence the reporter finally understood.

"You've never been back, have you?"

Rodney lifted his coffee cup and drank slowly, then set it down before raising his eyes to meet hers.

"No," he said. "Not yet."

It was opening night for *Christmas in Canaan*, and not surprisingly, the beautiful old Cullen Playhouse was filled. The advance notices for the play had been glowing. "A new Christmas classic," glowed one critic. "Rod Freeman cuts to the soul of the American heartland with humor and insight," raved another.

From his place in the front row of the balcony, his mother on one side, looking beautiful in her black evening gown, and his stepfather on the other, crisp in his dress uniform, Rodney settled back in his seat and tried to experience the play as someone else might, seeing it for the first time. It was never easy. There was just too much of the creator in the creation to ever laugh unexpectedly at a joke or feel a sudden pang of sadness or flush of anger the way an audience would. But tonight he found himself captivated and surprised by what he felt.

Perhaps it had to do with the performers. The actor who played Rodney was bright and likable. Wylie was darker—more menacing—than Rodney thought was necessary, and DJ came off with a snotty arrogance that made him hard to like at first, but gradually the power of the play began to tug at him, and he relaxed and let it carry him. As if for the first time he felt the sadness at the death of Miss Eunice, the despair of the failed harvest. He watched in awe at Daniel's determination to give them all a good Christmas.

"It's the first Christmas he'll have since his grandma died," Daniel was explaining to Wylie as Rodney huddled against the side of the barn, listening. "I want it to be special for him. For all of us."

Wylie wagged his head violently. If he was struggling

not to show too much anger, he was losing the battle. "We're lucky to have a roof over our heads. That Negro boy especially. Taking him in like he's a long-lost relative."

Hidden against the wall of the barn, the boy closed his eyes as the words hit home. In his seat in the front row of the balcony, the real Rodney did the same thing. He could feel the cold December air, smell the needles of the wrinkle pine. He could hear the resolute strength in Daniel's voice.

"We'll get by somehow. We always have."

Wylie exploded in anger, pounding the wall of the barn with his fist, and the boy staggered back as if he'd been shot. "And what if this is the year we don't? Answer me that! What if this is the year we can't get by? When you were dead set on takin' him in, I figured, now, that's your choice, even if it meant less for everybody. Now you're fixin' to gamble the farm . . . just to give that boy a fancy Christmas you can't afford. Sometimes I think you care more about that boy than you do about the rest of the family."

"He *is* the rest of the family," Daniel replied simply.

"Well," Wylie replied, "it's damn plain *you* think so."

With that, Wylie stormed off stage right, muttering to himself, as Rodney, remembering his mission, quickly entered the barn, picked up the bow saw from off its peg and silently disappeared stage left, leaving only Daniel, alone with his thoughts, center stage. He stood motionless as the lights slowly faded.

The applause was immediate and thunderous. Rodney opened his eyes just as the house lights came up for intermission. He could feel the energy around him, the sound an audience makes when they have been drawn into the story. Rodney had sensed it only a few times before and never for anything he had written, but this time it told him he had finally accomplished what he had being trying to accomplish all those years. He had taken this audience, these people, to a different place and time. To the land of milk and honey. He had taken them to Canaan.

The people laughed at the dilemma of the oversized Christmas tree and grew silent as Christmas Eve loomed and still there were no presents, but when the family opened their imaginary gifts, there was another sound in the darkened theater. Rodney could hear around him that telltale catch in the breathing, a muffled cough, a clearing of the throat, the collective sounds of people whose hearts had been touched by a simple truth. A truth that dwelt at the core of everything Daniel Burton believed: *love is made perfect only through sacrifice.*

In the end, they stood and cheered for curtain call after curtain call until finally, the boy who played Rodney pointed to the center seats in the front row of the balcony and a spotlight combed the crowd until it picked up Rodney. He stood and bowed to the cheering crowd, while those below craned their necks to get a glimpse of this young playwright who could so move them with his words.

Backstage the mood was exuberant, with bouquets of flowers arriving and champagne corks popping and guests dropping by to praise and celebrate and bask in the energy of a successful opening night. Photographers snapped photos and reporters scribbled notes as deliriously happy cast members talked excitedly about the play. Amid all the joy and laughter, nobody seemed to realize that the one person who had been responsible for creating it was nowhere to be seen. Rod Freeman had inexplicably vanished.

A lonely work light burned over the stage; otherwise, the Cullen Playhouse had retreated into the familiar silence of every darkened, empty theater, a cold muffled silence like winter. The rows of empty seats spread out like empty rows in a field. Or so it seemed to Rodney as he stood center stage and looked out into the darkness.

Remembering his mission, he reached into the breast pocket of his coat and gently tugged at something. It was an envelope, traveled and worn. Rodney studied it with reverence. As if he were handling an object of great value, he lifted the flap and carefully removed the contents. And there, in the quiet of that old theater, he stared at the clippings.

Bobby's red Stingray bicycle was on top.

Next was the fisherman working a mountain stream, wearing black waders and a fisherman's vest. In his hand a beautiful casting rod caught the glint of the morning sun. Everything that DJ had wanted.

And there was the clipping of a lovely pink sundress, worn by a willowy model with long hair that looked like it was made of spun gold as she stood against a sunset sky. Perfect for Sarah.

And for Wylie, the full-sized leather recliner, in which an older gentleman stretched out in obvious comfort as an attractive woman brought him a cocktail and slippers after a hard day on the golf course. Rodney smiled when he remembered how Wylie had growled when he saw it. There was little doubt that if he had ever sat in one, it would have been impossible to pry him out.

The last clipping was his. The portable typewriter complete with extra ribbons. Rodney hadn't kept it with the others, safe in the envelope. He had pinned it above his desk so he could see it night after night as he wrote into the small hours, struggling to find just the right word, and the next, and the next. Words that would end up as dialogue, and dialogue that would make up scenes. Scenes that would be collected into acts and, finally, completed plays. When he was hopelessly blocked and every word he wrote seemed wrong and he doubted if he would be able to finish even one sentence, he would stare at the small tattered picture pinned to his wall. Eventually the words he needed would come.

The sound of approaching footsteps echoing from the back of the empty theater cut short the memory, and Rodney turned and strained his eyes against the darkness.

"Hello?" he called.

"Mr. Freeman?" a voice said.

"Yes."

"Mr. Freeman? My name's Hansen," the voice replied. "Could I have a word with you?"

✴

Chapter Two

Christmas in Canaan

DJ barely slowed the old Ford as he and Bobby made the turn onto the long driveway. With spraying gravel and sounding horn, they approached the house and skidded to a stop in front as Daniel watched impatiently from the kitchen window all the while.

DJ looked even more like his father now that he was fully grown—tall, with broad shoulders and the same strong features. His hair had turned darker and he had filled out all of his six-foot frame, but there was still something very boyish about him. The rambling way he walked as if his legs were barely connected to his body. The mischievous look on his face when he sprung a joke on someone.

Bobby looked older, too. Despite the best rehabilitation therapy Daniel could afford, the injury to his back and legs had proved too severe and Bobby had come to accept, with a certain cheerful grace, that he would likely walk with crutches for the rest of his life.

The boys moved quickly toward the house, followed by Bandit, who moved a little slower and napped a little longer as each year passed.

"What took ya?" Daniel said. "You've been gone for hours."

"Ask him," DJ replied, indicating Bobby with a nod of his head.

"Had to find the perfect wrinkle pine," Bobby said. "Couldn't show up with the wrong one now, could we?"

"I reckon not," Daniel growled, peering out the kitchen window. The Ford was filled with a regal pine that seemed the size of a giant redwood. "Think that'll fit?"

Sarah didn't bother looking. "It'll have to." She picked up the basket of gingerbread and shooed the others toward the door. "Come on. We're late. Miss the bus and you're walking."

"Yeah, Dad, don't you remember?" DJ said. "Them's the rules."

"What rules? Who made that up?" Daniel grabbed his coat off the peg in the entry hall and headed for the door. "That's the silliest thing I ever heard. Did I ever make you walk to school?"

DJ had the truck started even before the others had climbed in. He, Daniel and Sarah crowded together in the cab, while Bobby held on to the tree with one hand and Bandit's collar with the other in the back. The tired transmission grinding into gear, the Burtons made their way down the long gravel drive leading to the county road.

"The radio mention snow?" Daniel asked, glancing with a hopeful eye out the window as DJ eased the pickup onto the dry blacktop.

"Nope," said DJ.

"Too bad. It'd be nice to have a dusting his first Christmas back."

✧ ✳ ✧

Twilight was settling as the old Ford slowed, crossed the narrow ditch and turned into the driveway leading back to Miss Eunice's house. The place hadn't changed at all since Rodney had left. DJ had kept his word about looking after the property, doing a lot of chores over the years, painting the porch, repairing the chimney and last spring replacing the screen door that had blown off its hinges. The only thing that had changed was the garden. DJ had planted some honeysuckle that had taken in a big way, filling the summer air with sweet perfume. He figured Miss Eunice would have liked to have something growing in the garden, even if it wasn't beans and corn and sweet potatoes.

Looking toward the house, Daniel could see that someone was home. A warm glow came from several of the windows, and a friendly curl of smoke rose from the chimney. As the pickup pulled to a stop in front of the house, there sat Rodney Freeman, waiting. He wore jeans and a comfortable wool sweater. Only the fine calfskin jacket and hand-tooled Tony Lama boots attested to his good fortune.

Bandit was the first out, barking excitedly at the sight of his old master.

"Hey, Bandit!" Rodney patted him and scratched behind his ears. "They feeding you okay? Are they, boy?"

DJ stepped down from the cab and grabbed Rodney, wrapping him in a bear hug and swinging him around like a bag of feed. "Well, look at you! Ain't you the city boy!"

Rodney laughed. "In California they think I'm a hick, and out here you think I look like a city boy. It's no wonder I spend half my time confused."

"I think you look wonderful." Sarah hugged him, stopping only long enough to take a good look at him before hugging him again.

"See?" said Rodney, giving DJ a knowing nod. "There's a woman who knows."

Bobby, balancing on his crutches, busily untied the ropes that lashed the tree to the bed of the truck.

"Hey, Bobber," Rodney called. "When'd you get so big?"

Bobby smiled. "I go by Bob now," he said. "I mean,

you can call me Bobber if you want." He nodded in the direction of the others. "It's just they can't. Not anymore."

"Bob's a good name. It suits you," he said. "It suits you fine."

Daniel had remained standing near the truck while the others were reunited. Why, he didn't exactly know. Something in him just wanted to savor the moment from afar. But it didn't last long. Seeing him standing there, Rodney crossed quickly to Daniel and threw his arms around him. "Merry Christmas, Mr. Burton," he said simply.

"Merry Christmas to you. Welcome home," Daniel answered.

Bobby freed the last rope. "Hey, come help with the tree," he called to the others, who turned just in time to watch it slide over the edge of the truck bed and hit the ground with a *thud*.

"That my tree?" Rodney asked doubtfully, his eyes sizing it up for the first time.

"Bet you can never guess who picked it out," DJ said,

rolling his eyes and throwing a nod in Bobby's direction. "Ol' Paul Bunyan there."

"Come on." Bobby ignored him, too busy trying to lift the tree with one hand and balance himself on his crutches with the other. "Let's get it inside!"

DJ sighed. It was inevitable and he knew it. He lifted and shouldered the trunk while Rodney tugged on the top. Grudgingly the tree moved across the driveway while the others followed along in single file. The procession had nearly reached the porch steps when suddenly Rodney stopped and set down his end of the wrinkle pine.

"You all right?" DJ asked.

"I'm fine. I just remembered. There's one more thing that needs doing," Rodney said. He reached into his pocket, and out came the well-traveled envelope. As they watched, he opened it and held up the clippings for them to see. "I've been hauling these things around with me all these years," explained Rodney. "Thought you might like to have 'em back.

Sarah gasped. "It's 'some' Christmas."

As they huddled on the porch of Miss Eunice's house, Rodney handed each of them a clipping. The bicycle to Bobby. The fishing gear to DJ. The beautiful sundress to Sarah. And Wylie's recliner he gave to Daniel. Each accepted the clipping with a hushed reverence, as if the magic of *some* Christmas were still somehow embodied in those small worn images.

"I kept them to remind me of a promise I made myself the last Christmas I was in Canaan, a promise I planned to keep my first Christmas *back* in Canaan. I reckon that's now."

Rodney crossed to the front door and swung it open. The light from inside bathed their faces in a rich golden glow as they stared in amazement. The front room of Miss Eunice's was filled with gifts, the most wonderful gifts imaginable, since they were the very gifts Daniel had imagined in his heart so many years before.

Not that they were exactly the same. Instead of a bicycle, a bright red motor scooter, complete with a red bow on top, sat prominently in the center of the room, along with helmet and gloves. Next to the scooter sat an enormous tan recliner and matching ottoman, the luster of the supple Italian leather warmed by the lamplight. Along one wall hung not only a lovely pink sundress like the one in the clipping, but an array of dresses and silk blouses and cashmere sweaters, handmade shoes from Italy and handbags from the Champs-Élysées, their buckles reflecting the glow from nearby candles. Along the other wall hung a complete set of fishing equipment. Waders. Hats. A tackle box. A series of bait rods and fly rods and next to them, standing on end and barely able to fit in the room, a small aluminum boat with outboard motor. The rest of the room was filled with lamps and lanterns and candles, making everything shimmer and dance in the enchanted light.

They stood motionless, staring through the door at the wonderland of gifts. They might have stayed outside all night if Rodney hadn't urged them in.

"Come on," he said, his voice barely able to contain his delight at their surprise. "Don'tcha want to have 'some' Christmas?"

Still they didn't move.

317

Bobby was the first to speak. "You know this tree we brought? It ain't gonna fit."

Rodney ushered them into the house and stood back to let them discover the gifts for themselves.

DJ slowly fingered one of the fly rods carefully, testing the action as Rodney watched.

"Don't know if you'll catch anything, but you'll look great trying," Rodney said.

Behind him, Bobby sat astride the motor scooter, his gloves and helmet strapped tightly on, fiddling with the controls as Rodney wandered by.

"Sorry they don't make Stingrays anymore, but at least it's got an automatic so you don't have to worry about shifting. The man said it should do sixty."

"I bet it'll do eighty," Bobby said.

"You think?"

"I know it'll do eighty. Easy."

In the corner of the room, Sarah was holding up the blouses, trying to catch a glimpse of her reflection in the windows.

"There's a mirror in the bedroom," Rodney said.

"I don't want to leave," Sarah gasped. "What if I leave and it all disappears? What if it's only a dream?"

"In a dream, you don't worry that it's a dream," said Rodney, but Sarah didn't seem convinced.

She held up a dress. It was washed silk in a rich blue, expertly cut on the bias so that it ended in a pleasing ruffle.

"It's beautiful," Sarah whispered, barely able to get the words out. "How did you know my size?"

"Why do you think I kept callin' you up, asking about women's dress sizes?"

"You said you needed it for a show you were doing."

Rodney beamed. "You don't call *this* a show? Besides, there's a persistent rumor I've been hearing ever since I hit town about this ambitious young county surveyor up in Clarksboro who seems to be spending most of his free time surveying the road in front of the Jerrit place. I wanted you to look especially nice in case he got lost and wandered up to the door."

"His name is James W. Thomas," Sarah said. Then, leaning over to Rodney, she added in a whisper, "I think he's going to ask me to marry him."

"You're getting married?" Rodney exclaimed.

"Shhh!" Sarah blushed deeply. "I'm not supposed to tell anyone. Not yet. But I had to tell someone."

"Don't worry," Rodney answered. "I'm pretty good at keeping secrets."

Daniel had taken refuge in the new leather recliner, watching the joyous discovery happening in all directions around him, but the leather proved so supple, he closed his eyes and leaned back.

"Top-grain Italian leather. Therapeutic heat. Dual massage motors."

Daniel looked up to see Rodney standing at the foot of the chair. Daniel smiled and shook his head.

"Wylie woulda loved this. He'd have parked himself in it and we'd never have gotten him out." He gripped the armrest and lowered the chair into the fully reclined position and settled in for a moment, his pleasure and comfort obvious. But the memories of Wylie had also produced a little pull of sadness. "It's thoughtful of you, remembering him like this. He'd be very pleased."

"There's something else," Rodney said, leaning close so

no one else could hear. "I need to talk to you. In the kitchen."

The kitchen was filled with everything imaginable for a Christmas feast, every square inch of its meager counter space covered with festive holiday dishes. From the oven wafted the heavenly aroma of the turkey that Aunt Celie had been roasting all afternoon and had left with explicit instructions for serving. Daniel waited expectantly as Rodney closed the kitchen door. Reaching into his pocket, he handed the farmer a business card. "I want you to call this man," he said.

Daniel read the card aloud. "Dr. Wayne Hansen, Orthopedic Surgeon." He stopped, looked up sharply.

"He read about me in the paper. An interview I gave in the *Chronicle*. I told about the fire and how Bobby tried to warn everyone. And about the accident. He came to my play just to meet me."

Daniel shook his head. He had heard enough to imagine where this was heading. "We done the best we could for him. I can't afford to try another doctor."

"This man's a teacher. At Stanford University. He says

there're some new things they can do for people with Bobber's injury. New techniques. He thinks maybe he can help."

Again Daniel shook his head, more sadly than before. "I reckon that'd cost more money than I'm likely to see the rest of my life," Daniel sighed, unable to conceal the effects of years of frustration. Remembering the mountain of expenses, and the hopes that sprang up, only to be dashed. He turned to the window, where the last gray of twilight had all but faded.

Rodney crossed to where he stood and, placing his hands on Daniel's shoulders, turned him back until they were face-to-face. "You don't understand. It won't cost anything. He's offered to do it for free."

"Free?" Daniel exclaimed, as if the whole notion reeked of charity.

"As part of his research. He'll even fly Bobber out to California. All you have to do is come along."

"He'd do it for free?" Daniel questioned, stubbornly refusing to consider the idea. "I don't understand. Why would some fella offer to do that? Offer to help some kid he doesn't even know? For free? I don't get it."

Rodney smiled. "Now that's a good question, isn't it?"

Daniel looked up into the face of this young man, so bright, so full of promise, a face that could barely contain its joy at the irony unfolding before them.

"That's what I always wanted to know. Why would some fella be willing to do something that generous for a kid he doesn't even know?" Rodney asked. "Have to say I'm surprised, Mr. Burton. Of all the people on the face of the earth," he said, his voice softening, "I figured if anyone knew the answer to that one, it'd be you."

They gathered around a table covered with the most beautiful spread anyone could remember. There were baked yams with browned marshmallows and velvety cheesed onions and fresh snap beans with slivered almonds and individual dishes filled with cranberry relish. In the center sat the turkey, golden brown, spilling its load of cornbread-and-sausage dressing. There was barely enough room to fit it all on the table.

Rodney, seated at the head of the table, made a simple

request. "Mr. Burton," he asked. "will you say grace?"

Daniel thought for a moment before he kindly shook his head. "No," he said. "Sayin' grace is reserved for the head of the house. Especially on Christmas. Them's the rules."

"Well," Rodney said. "I guess if them's the rules . . ." Around Miss Eunice's table, the very table at which she had offered grace for so many years, with heads bowed and hands clasped, they waited for the blessing.

"We thank thee, Heavenly Father," Rodney began, "for this food that's been prepared for the nourishment of our bodies." He paused for the briefest of moments, wanting to remember the words exactly as he first heard Wylie pray them. "Help us to spend the strength that we derive from it in doing good . . . and in keeping thy commandments. Amen."

"Amen," the others responded, followed by Daniel, a second later, his voice soft with gratitude.

"Amen," he said.

As serving dishes were passed and plates filled, stories told and laughter shared, everyone pressed around the table agreed there would never be another Christmas in Canaan like this one. But silently, within each heart, there was a deeper understanding—as long as there was family, there would always be *some* Christmas. Daniel had proven that.

Outside, the first few flakes of snow silently appeared, floating slowly down, but only Bandit seemed to notice. He barked and snapped at a few lazy flakes before settling back where it was warm, tucked amid the boughs of the wrinkle pine resting on the front steps of the old Freeman place, just where Bobby had left it.

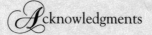Acknowledgments

We would like to thank Morgan Farley for her keen insights and guidance; Katherine Brown Tegen for her great instincts and editorial skill in shaping the story; Doug Dean and Carol Richardson for their tireless support; and, of course, Lew Weitzman and Al Zuckerman.